Klail City

A Novel

Rolando Hinojosa

Arte Público Press
Houston

This volume is made possible through support from the National Endowment for the Arts, a federal agency, and the Texas Commission on the Arts.

Arte Público Press
University of Houston
University Park
Houston, Texas 77004

Library of Congress No. 85-073353
ISBN 0-934770-54-9

Printed in the United States of America

The book is dedicated to Rory, Kathi, and to Jim Lee, Tom Pilkington, my colleague Don Graham, Lonnie Bannon, the proposition that men are created, my late brother Roy Lee, my older brother Rene, and to my friend Tomás Rivera and his memory.

The book is also dedicated to my two sisters, Clarissa and Dora Mae, and to another writer: a nephew of mine called Eddie who once wondered aloud why I wasted so much of my time. He now knows I wasn't wasting it; and, he also knows why we enjoyed the bullfights so much: it was the drinking that went along with them.

A long dedication and long in coming and thus overdue. A person who has no place to call home, who has no friends or relatives can still do many things on earth. Many things. But, he can't be a writer; not for long, at any rate.

It took me a long time to find this out for myself.

Also by the author:

Estampas del valle y otras obras

Klail City y sus alrededores

Korean Love Songs

Mi querido Rafa

Rites and Witnesses

The Valley

Dear Rafe

Partners in Crime

Claros varones de Belken/Fair Gentlemen of Belken County

Klail City:

A Novel

Prologue

As usual, this writer has made use of friends to help him tell his story; he has also made use of several devices, several techniques. Nothing startling, however. He needed them, and he took them.

He has also made use of three narrators: Rafe Buenrostro, Jehu Malacara, and P. Galindo, to help him in the telling of this edition of the Belken County Chronicles of the Death Trip Series. The writer needs all the help he can come up with, by the way. This last shouldn't be taken as an apology or as a form of one; show me a writer who goes around apologizing, and I'll show you a writer in trouble. The literature doesn't need an apology either; show me a literature that does and so on . . .

Three narrators and a cast of hundreds; of the latter, most go around asking why they were put on this earth. The former know full well; and, they know better than to ask.

It's always been that way; nothing new. Now, this writer doesn't live in a cave, by the by. And so, he has also heard of people who claim to have been born again. This writer finds that hard to take, let alone swallow. The writer attributes this attitude to his upbringing and to his father, a man of long intellect but of very short fuses. This writer also notes that those people don't talk about resurrection after three days; at least not yet, anyway.

This, of course, reminds him of a story concerning his father:

My father had heard of a neighbor who claimed to have been reborn, and he went out to see this real, substantial, first class, genuine miracle and came back with the following report:

"I liked the old one better; he didn't talk as much."

The same could be said about this writer's books; they say what they have to say and then get the hell out of everyone's way.

That's fair enough, isn't it?

Time Marked and Time Bided

Well now, some of the taxpayers to be seen in Klail City have appeared on other occasions and at other times; in times past, some have scarcely been mentioned at all, and then, of course, there are those who are coming out for the first time; making their debut, as it were.

The number of Texas Anglos to be seen here is scant, but perhaps, understandably so. These fellow Texans of ours are out of place here; out of their element, so to speak. So to speak.

The Belken County Texas Mexicans, on the other hand, are in the majority, but this doesn't mean they ignore the other population; they can ill afford to do so. For their part, the mexicanos are usually ignored, although not always, true, and not forever either. (After all, what physical pain is there that lasts a hundred years?)

Caveat: one shouldn't expect to find legendary heroes here; our taxpayers go to the toilet on a regular basis, sneeze on cue and blow their noses too, as the limerick says. Some raise families, and most of them know Death well enough, but (innocents that they are) they don't pretend to know what it is that usually happens to them *after* death. As a rule, the Texas Mexican, being a Texan, is a hard nut to crack, and this will be seen enough and throughout.

But, back to the heroes for a moment: the reader who looks here for a hero on the order of, say, Ruy Díaz, el Cid (the son of Diego Lainez) will be given short shrift. That reader, simply put, is baying up the wrong mesquite tree: there's nothing there for him to hunt. No heroes, then, although the reader knows, senses, suspects that there are certain and definite ways of being heroic. Showing up for work (and doing it) and then putting up with whatever fool happens to come bobbing along is no laughing matter.

Thus, by refusing to break, by working hard at living and letting live, and neither quitting nor faltering, the mexicano folk know, in great part, what life is like and about. Whatever else is left (a Sunday sermon, say) is hard to take when the pews are wooden and unpaid for, as we say.

Putting up (cf. Resistance) may be genetic; congenital, even. As Don Quijote says: "Anything is possible." It could, of course, be something else; it could be a legitimate product of living and working and putting up day after day with one's fellow citizens. In short, individual and communal heroism calls for patience and forbearance. This makes for a more interesting life, by the way.

And now, on to Klail City (and other places) (here and there).

The Tamez Family

Don Servando, dau. and sons:
Joaquín
Ernesto
Berta, and
Jovita, Don Servando's dau.-in-law-to-be.

Here we go. Jovita ue Anda is pregnant, and Joaquín Tamez, the eldest of the three Tamez brothers, has rightfully owned up to it. The outcome to all of this? The truth is one never knows.

*   *   *

"No! No! No! And not only No, but *Hell* no!"

"Pa, the thing is . . ."

"That's enough, Bertie; you stay out of this. Go on, out to the yard now and leave us alone."

"All right, Pa . . ."

"You, Emilio, . . . over here."

"Yessir, Pa."

"You go tell don Manuel Guzmán that we're doing all right here, and that there isn't going to be trouble, either. All you have to say is that Joaquín and Jovita are getting married this afternoon. And then you ask him—*ask*, got that?—you ask him that he look in on the de Anda family. We don't want any trouble from that end of it."

"Oh, yeah? Why do we have to *ask* anybody?"

"Joaquín, I'm going to say this the one time: shut-the-hell-up. You, Emilio! Any questions?"

"No, Pa; none at all, no."

"On your way, then. Ah, hold it a minute . . ."

"Huh?"

"When you get back, I want you to stand out there, across the street."

"Sure thing, Pa; be right back."

* * *

"Jovita . . ."

"Yessir . . ."

"That door there leads to my wife's room; Joaquín was born there and so was Emilio and Ernesto and Bertie-Babe. And, my wife died there. Now, you go on in there and sit on the bed; don't open the door until I say so."

"Yessir . . ."

"Now, you two come with me to the kitchen."

* * *

"Couldn't wait, could you? Just had to pull 'em down, didn't you? And now what? This! Good God Almighty, Joaquín . . ."

"Look, Pa, we . . ."

"No; I'm not looking, and I'm not listening, either. No sir."

"But I . . . Pa, you know we want to get married, don't you?

"Yes, but not like this, Joaquín. I sure as hell didn't want it like this at all. No sir. I wanted things done right, dammit. And I'll tell you why right now: your sister, our Bertie. How do you think she's going to feel at school when her friends . . . .

"Aw, go on, Pa . . ."

"Well, look who's talking all of a sudden, Ernesto the Mute. Small wonder it wasn't you who . . . Look at me! Neto, one of these days young Cordero's going to bring you up short on account of that sister of his. No! Don't say a

12

word, Ernesto. And when he does, he's . . ."

"Nah, he won't do a thing; he'll chicken out, he . . ."

"And that's where You. Are. Wrong. As. All. Hell."

"Joaquín's right, Ernesto. Young Cordero's tough enough when he has to be, and he's no coward."

"Pa, you still say we're not going to invite the de Andas?"

"Joaquín, I said *no*, and I meant *no*. So, which *word* didn't you understand?"

"But, Pa, Jovita happens to . . ."

"For the last time, Joaquín, neither you nor Jovita have a word to say in any of this. You hang on to that. You two are getting married here. In this house. In that very room where your mother died, and to hell with the witnesses. Ernesto brings the justice of the peace, right here, and that's it. Emilio'll stay out there, the judge and us in here, and you and Jovita marry up, and that's all there is to it."

"And what if the de Andas show up? Then what?"

"They won't! Now, old don Marcial de Anda might want to come over, but he won't, and I know he won't. Oh, he'll cry and carry on, but that's as far as it'll go."

"Okay, Pa, but it's going on two o'clock."

"Fine. Joaquín, go to the back door and call your sister in; tell her to wait with Jovita in your Mom's room."

"Okay, Pa . . . when's Neto going for the J.P.?"

"Now; right now. Ernesto, don't you be stopping anywhere along the way. You got that? I want you back here before three o'clock . . . Go on, move it."

"But what if the Judge's not at home?"

"He'll be there."

"But if he ain't, then what?"

"I said he'd be there, go on, now."

"But if he ain't?"

"GOD-DAMMIT-TO-HELL! Just what . . .?"

"Hold on, Pa; I didn't mean . . ."

"Look Neto, I've always given you more rope than the

others 'cause you're the youngest and because I promised your Ma I would, but one of these days, I'm going to give you a hiding like you won't forget. You may be twenty-three years old and all, but you're not too old for me to take the whip to."

"What's going on, Pa?"

"Nothing, Bertie; don't worry about it now. Go join Jovita, hon, she's in your Mom's room."

* * *

"Pa, it's a bit galling, Pa . . . I mean, you, ah, you take a lot-a guff from Neto, you know that? Shoot. If either Emilio or I'd talk to you the way *he* does, why, you'd pin our ears back, and they'd stay pinned, too . . . And it's Neto's fault, Pa . . . He's a pain in the ass, Pa . . . Emilio and I are forever getting him out-a scrapes and all. But does he worry? Not him, no sir."

"Listen to me, Joaquín, this house and everything in it is all we got, but it's ours. And when I die, you'll be in charge. So . . ."

"Yeah, I know, I'll be in charge."

"That's right, the one in charge. Ernesto'll have to get along, and he will, don't you worry about that end of it. Now, as for you, well, you're about to be a married man, you'll have to be responsible for the house, Bertie, and . . . she's growing up, you know. First thing'll happen, why, she'll run off, elope . . . She's eighteen or nineteen, you know . . ."

"Not her, Pa."

"Hmph! Listen to what I'm saying. You keep an eye out. We're not raising her to be no old maid, but I don't want her winding up like Jovita there . . ."

"Gee, Pa, she'll hear you, they both will."

"Let 'em, and I want Bertie to hear me. As for Jovita, her case is settled: you two'll be married inside the hour, and that's it. She's going to live here; this is her home now."

14

"Look out the window, Pa. There's Emilio coming up. Want me to call him in?"

"No, he's staying out there. Okay, you're going to be a married man, so cut out the fartin' around, and that's my last word on that. Now, go call the girls and we'll wait for the judge here."

* * *

And that's what happened. Jovita de Anda and Joaquín Tamez became man and wife; a family affair that wedding: small, private, sober. The de Andas (quiet, hardworking, industrious, and meek) went along and stayed away. That last wasn't their choice, but stay away they did. Jovita was legally married, and that was the important thing.

The neighborhood had itself a time talking about it, but, as usual, the topic was dropped and soon forgotten; nothing new. As time went on, however, Jovita did deliver, and it was a baby girl; a beauty, according to don Servando. Baptized and christened, the baby was named for her paternal grandmother: Gertrudis. Don Servando gained a few years of life on that, and he's still around, giving hell and taking none.

A lot of folks on both sides of the tracks bruit about (in low tones) that the Tamez family is loud, disgraceful, etc. But, to date, no one's picked up the first stone.

For the record: The Tamezes pay their debts on time; they're not about to start suffering fools gladly; and they work like dray horses: hard, steady, and for the long pull.

Echevarría Has the Floor

A. Choche Markham: A Cantina Monologue

B. Doña Sóstenes

C. The Buenrostro-Leguizamón Affair.

a. The Dogs Are Howling

Choche Markham:
A Cantina Monologue

Our friend, is he? A champion of the Texas Mexican, you say? Well! When did this come about? What splendid, glorious—miraculous—transformation have we witnessed here? A friend? *Choche* Markham? Ha!

Has that word been so devalued that he can fit it and wear it like a glove? Choche Markham a *friend*? My Gawd, people! Is there no such thing as memory?

Was splitting Olegario Gamez's skull with a Colt .45 the action of a *friend*? Well? Go on, somebody: explain *that* piece of business to me, goddammit! Friend!

The man's a coward. To the core! And when it comes to *nerve*, ha! *Nerves* is more like it. Friend! Don't you call *me* friend, no, not if you use it on him. No sir.

Remember those bullocks on the Carrizal land? Big-footed, heavy, lumbering, and not worth doodley-squat? Overgrown pieces of absolute shit, right? Well, that's our man, Choche Markham, yeah. That fine, fair friend of the mexicano people! And if you don't *think* he's your friend, just ask him. Yeah; what better authority could you want?

Well? What happens when don Manuel Guzmán comes into this or any other cantina in Klail? Well? That's right: things get peaceful like, don't they? And if they don't, he'll make damn sure they get quiet. But he won't pull that gun out, and he sure as hell doesn't take you outside, point his finger at you, embarrass you . . . Hell no! But what about our *dear* friend, Choche Markham? Piece of Texas rinche shit. Damright. Outside, where people'll see him.

And listen to this: he's married to a mexicana, did-you-know-that? And how does he treat her? Well? Ha! ¡Qué chingaos!

But family aside, now. The Texas Anglo still thinks that the *rinches* hung that goddam moon up there. That they're tougher than tarred-up cedar posts. Yeah? Well what the hell happened in the Ambrosio Mora shooting? Young Mora was unarmed. That's right! Van Meers shot young Mora—right there—across those tracks, by the J.C. Penney Store, on a Palm Sunday afternoon as the song says. And you know what? A thousand and one goddam people saw it. And? So? Listen to this: three years! It took the state of Texas three years to get the case going, and when it did, what happened? Well, now: here comes old Choche Markham—that great and good friend of ours—yeah, he came over and he swore in as a witness for Deputy Van Meers! For the man who did the shooting and the killing, for Christ's sakes! Jesus, people! . . . Hmph, and I'll tell you this, too, there are still mexicanos up and down this crazy Valley of ours who say that Choche Markham is our friend! Gaaaaaaa-Damn! How many more examples do they want? Do we need?

I don't know, people, really, I don't . . . Are we *that* dumb? Are we *really* that dumb? Is that why we are *where* we are? I mean, if we're among God's dumbest creatures, then let's quit shittin' ourselves and let's admit it. Let's buy the rope for 'em, tie the goddam thing 'round our necks, hand it to them and say, "Go ahead, yank it!"

Well, I say we're *not* dumb. We're foolish as hell sometimes, we can't agree at other times, and we don't even like each other very much either, but Lord Jesus help us, we should *at least* know who the hell the enemy is when we see him.

God . . . The trouble is, it's been going on for years . . . . Before young Rafe Buenrostro here was out-a short pants. When your Dad was killed, son. Yeah. There're some people in this cantina this afternoon who remember that. Yes they do.

And what did Choche Markham—that knight in shining armor—that loving heart, that ball-breaking, Mexican-hating son-of-a-bitch do? Balls! You know what he said, though: "I'll clear it up; I'll get to the bottom of this."

That's what he *said*. Know what he *did*? He scratched his ass, picked his nose and then scratched his ass again. Well, hell! I can do that, and I don't even carry a badge *or* a gun. Now, you know what happened . . . don Julián Buenrostro went after his brother's killers, and they were killers for hire; they were from across the Río, and they didn't even know who it was they were killing. Didn't care, either; that kind never does: it was for money, see?

Well, they sure as hell didn't spend much of that money 'cause don Julián caught 'em and did 'em in: just-like-that. And he went *alone*, and that's something our hero Choche Markham just can't *do*, he'll never go alone. No sir.

And get this. He draws his pay from the State, all right, but you can't tell me that the Leguizamón family don't slip him some money now and again! That's *right*.

Choche Markham! Some friend; yeah, sure. Why, if I had any money, I'd give you five, ten, fifteen dollars to show me when and where it was he helped a mexicano . . . and I mean Mexicans other than the kind we all know about. Those mexicanos have been bought and sold so many times, for so many things, by so many people, for oh! so goddam long that they're *nothing* now. They don't even know *what* they are . . .

But don't kid yourselves about Choche Markham, whatever else you may do. Right . . . You forget once, and you'll wind up like those *vendidos*, those bought-and-sold-out lumps of caca-shit-mierda eaters. *Pendejos, babosos* . . .

Aw, what the hell . . . .

Doña Sóstenes

(About the time I returned from Korea) Doña Sóstenes Jasso, widow to Capt. Carmona, must have been about sixty-five-years old and widowed for some forty-odd of those sixty-five years.

The widowhood was the handiwork of José Isabel Chávez, a baby-faced, freebooting guerrilla leader who lined up Mexican Army regular Jacinto Carmona (Capt., Cav.) against a wall in Parangaracutiro, Michoacán and ordered him shot along with eleven others in Carmona's mounted patrol. Doña Sóstenes and her sister Herminia came to Klail City in 1915; Herminia, the younger of the two, became my Uncle Julián's first wife. Me, I was bartending during the summers at Lucas Barrón's place, the *Aquí me quedo** when one day doña Sóstenes walked by, grandson in tow, as I was serving Esteban Echevarría a cold Falstaff.

A beer, Rafe; just the one more I need to get going here. I've got a good head of steam, boys, so step aside . . . . Sóstenes, Sóstenes, I'm one of the ones who knew you when, yes I am, and I can say it again: *I knew you when . . .*

Ours is an old generation, boys, even though I got her beat by some twenty years there; I first saw her and that sister of hers back in '17 or '18, I think it was; at any rate, it was right before they paved the streets here in Klail, and she wasn't skinny then, boys, and she wasn't dried up either. No sir. That widow of Cavalry Captain Carmona was a traffic stopper; yes, those were the days, Sóstenes girl, and I knew you when, didn't I?

Well, sir, it just so happens that when Jacinto Carmona together with his horses and men fell into that trap laid out by the guerrilla Chávez, Carmona's wife was living in the Car-

---

*Lucas Barrón is also known as Dirty Luke.

mona family homestead in Doctor Cos, Nuevo León. That telegram giving her the terrible news was sent out two months later, and then, she didn't get the wire itself until three weeks after it got to town. In short, Sóstenes, times being what they were, had been a widow the whole of the summer of '14, without her knowing it. News, good or bad, just didn't travel fast in those days; it was another time, boys . . .

Well, as I was saying, she and her sister got to Klail in '15 or so, and they were first helped out by don Manuel Guzmán's wife; didn't know 'em, of course, just saw 'em and took 'em in. The sisters needed help, and that was enough for Josefa Guzmán. And they stayed there, too, least ways until Herminia married don Julián Buenrostro . . . Did you know that, Rafe?

"Yes."

Now, where was I? Oh, yeah. Anyway, in those days when women started wearing shorter skirts and dresses, the Jasso women kept the long ones, but shave my hair and call me Baldy: long skirts or no, we're talking of first-class goods here, top-a-the line merchandise. Yessir!

Now, when some of the gang here learned that the oldest one was a widow, some of 'em started getting all sort-a ideas. But they couldn't have been more out of true if they tried. Nothing.

Not even the faintest angel's breath of hope, no sir. Then, a year or so later, Herminia marries up with don Julián at the Carmen Ranch and Sóstenes moves right in. Now, had she— just by chance let's say—had she stayed here in Klail, maybe nothing would've happened; no way to tell now, of course, and maybe . . . well, lemme just back up a bit here . . .

"Echevarría! Stay on course!"

Right where I'm at, Turnio; just checkin' the riggin' and the sails, is all . . . Well, sir, Sóstenes went off to the Carmen Ranch, and it was there that Melesio Parra, the eldest of Melesio Senior's bunch—the ones that still run that dairy farm there—and Antonio Cruz, a short little old runt raised by the

Archuletas, remember those New Mexicans who moved in here? Well, it was at the Carmen Ranch where those two youngsters shot and killed each other right to death and all for Sóstenes. Damfools.

That's right, just-like-that . . . shot themselves full-a holes, they did. And for what, I ask you? Ah, for Sóstenes's love . . . Ha! For Sóstenes's love . . . And will you look at 'er now . . . old, gray-haired, wrinkly, bent over by all those years, and to think—like the tango says—and to think that life's a puff of breath and little else . . . ha!

But that was it . . . they just shot and killed each other, and the widow didn't know a thing about it. It's enough to make you laugh or cry, one . . . She didn't even *know* them, hadn't laid *eyes* on 'em. Ever. They were the ones who got it into their heads that they were rivals. I mean, she had absolutely no idea . . .

Ahhhh, but you know how it always is: the crowd said that fault and blame had to be placed on a woman. Yeah. Convenient, even if I say so. But hang on to this: they died, they stayed dead, and they're not coming back. Uh-uh . . .

Shoot! Sóstenes wasn't a dishrag to be picked up and rubbed and squeezed and laid out by just anyone who happened to come along. No sir. She wasn't even at the dance when those two went at it. And you know *what*? The dance was being held right at the Carmen Ranch itself, but she didn't go to 'em. Anywhere. Period.

Young Parra and the Cruz boy killed themselves, and that was it. That other people came by later on and said *she* was to blame, well, that was someone's tongue working back and forth, and that was it, because as far as she was concerned: nothing. Right, Maistro?

"God's truth and no one else's, Echevarría. It was one of those dances organized by María Lara . . ."

"María Lara? That old sack fulla-bones?"

"You youngsters don't know what you're talking about."

"Echevarría's had too much to drink!"

"Yeah? Well, he pays his own way."

"Keep it down . . . go on, Echevarría."

Nothing to it, boys . . . I saw Sóstenes go by, and I thought about the old days; when she was young. That's all.

"See what you guys've done now?"

"Don't mind 'em, Echevarría. Can I buy you a beer?"

"Go on, Echevarría; don't pay 'em no mind."

Well, lemme ask Rafe here. You think I'm drunk?

"No."

And would you sell me a beer right now?

"Anytime."

Let's hear it for the Buenrostros, goddammit. Rafe, make this one a Falstaff.

*　*　*

"Oh, I remember it, all right . . . Young Parra's gun was one-a them Ivory-Johnson's, the kind you break open in the middle. But it wasn't his. The damn thing belonged to his brother-in-law, Tomás Arreola."

"And the other guy?"

"No, that gun was his, all right. A .38. And, it was just like Esteban Echevarría said it was: face to face, pistol in hand."

"And like real men, and all that old stuff, right?"

"Yeah, it was a damfool thing to do."

"And Echevarría was there? He saw it all?"

"Oh, yeah; we both did. We must've gone there together that night . . . As for Sóstenes, well, she received—and she still may, you know—a smallish pension from the Mexican government on account of her husbad's being a regular army officer."

"I can't imagine the pension's all that much; do you?"

"No, probably not."

"But regular as the sunset, I bet."

23

"So then what happened between the two families, the Parras and the Cruz bunch?"

"Oh, it worked out all right. It started and ended there, with those two."

"That was a stroke of luck."

"But to kill each other for someone like that . . ."

"Well, she wasn't like *that*, then . . ."

"Yeah, I know, but still 'n all, it was a damfool thing to do."

Ho! Rafe, I gotta be going.

"See you tomorrow, Echevarría."

God hear you.

The Buenrostro-Leguizamón Affair

Graffiti at Dirty Luke's:

Dirty Linen Had Damn Well Better Be Washed
  at Home.

Nosey Neighbors Need a Nose Job.

The Hard of Hearing Should Learn to Lip-Read.

When it Comes to the Law: Mum's the Word.

The Losers of the World Need a Shorter Bridge to
  Walk On.

Meddling is Asking for Trouble on Credit.

Echevarría is standing at the end of the *Aquí me Quedo Bar*;
he jumps to the bar, sits down, and says he has decided to tell
(once and for all) what he knows about the death, years ago,
of don Jesús Buenrostro.

Echevarría says he meets the necessary requirements: a
clear memory, the brio, and the desire. As he says: "Nothing
to it, once you know."

Yesterday, boys . . . as if it were yesterday, I tell you. I
remember it well, and I remember don Jesús, *el quieto*, a
straighter arrow I never saw; a good man. I know young
Rafe's here with us, but I'd say the same whether he was here
or not. Ha! I've known this boy since the day he was born and
baptized; I knew his Dad, his uncle, too, and all that fine
hard-working bunch from the Carmen Ranch; yessir.

Now: I know, yes, I do, I know and own up that whenever I get drunk, you-all start shucking and husking at me . . . But you also know I put up with it, and I'll tell you why: I put up because I also know that the best thing to do is to shut the hell up . . . but only if I can't put up. You got that? But will you look at me now? And look at the time on that wall there; not one drink, not before, and not now . . .

(Young Murillo, don Víctor Solís's son-in-law, has paid for a round of drinks and breaks in on Echevarría, but does so with respect: "You've got the floor, Echevarría. All right, everybody, give 'im room.")

As I was saying just now: I remember as if it were yesterday, and I can still see don Jesús *el quieto* working and defending those lands of his at El Rancho Carmen. The Rangers had finally stopped bothering us borderers for a while, and all the ranches were at peace with the world. The uneasiness was still there, and so was the rancor, but things had abated somewhat, and now it looked as if the mexicano people could concentrate on living and on working for that living.

Now, your fathers and your grandfathers can still remember some of these doings and comings and goings, and they knew, sure they did, they knew that the Troubles weren't over yet, or that they could never be over until the Buenrostros and the Leguizamóns made their peace—or until both families disappeared from God's favorite planet.

And time went on and by, that summer, a second summer, and still no peace. The U.S. Army showed up, too, but weddings were held, and both the land and the women were harvested, and the mexicanos from Belken County watched and waited and counted every step they took: ever watchful, and waiting for the other shoe. But the rancor prevailed, and it was the Leguizamóns who again took the first step: they armed themselves with the sheriff and an attorney or two, and they showed up at the Buenrostro land, all formal-like.

For their part, the Buenrostros were ready: 'Here're the

papers, look them over, and thank you kindly. There'll be somebody to show you out on the East Gate when you're through here.'

Frustrated, the Leguizamóns started buying up some more land and so much so that the Carmen Ranch was almost cut off from some good Rio Grande River water. The Buenrostros worked but that's not all they did: they began posting guards and arming them just in case a cow wandered off somewhere, don't you know . . .

It'd been a hot spring, and a dry one, to boot; despite that though, the orange blossoms were trying their best to bloom out-a the buds, and it was on an April evening that someone sneaked up and murdered don Jesús . . . while the man slept, but this you already know, Rafe. But the *matones*, the killers, they were scared off by don Julián who happened to be riding the fences that night; the *matones* were trying to burn the tarps and don Jesús along with them, too, when don Julián came riding up the camp fire; the backshooters must've heard the horse 'cause they just backed out into the dark here . . .

Don Julián, without a word, took his brother's body and began to dig a grave at the foot of that big ol' Texas pecan tree; and the tree's still there, as a witness . . . the family gath . . .

Echevarría stops and turns aside. The crowd is waiting for the old man to go on. Suddenly, Young Murillo shouts out: "Don Esteban, don Esteban, go on, don . . ."

A shake of the head.

Tableau: Echevarría, back to crowd has a hand on the double-swing doors; the crowd, expectantly, rises and stares at the old man; Rafe Buenrostro stares at the floor . . .

The Dogs are Howling

"Sh . . . sh . . . sh . . . Quiet, Nieves. Listen now. Can you hear them? Don't you hear the dogs out there? Sh, sh, they're a long way off, across the lake there. Do you, can you hear 'em?"

"Well, I . . . you think . . ."

"Sh, sh, there they go again. Can you hear them now, by the Buenrostro side?"

"Yes, now I do. What is it, Esteban? What does it mean?"

"Sh. Listen . . . I even thought I heard a shot, maybe two . . . I was half-awake, I think; tossing, turning, and then I heard something or I thought I did. Yeah . . . and then the dogs, far away . . ."

"There they are again, Esteban."

"You *can* hear them, can't you?"

"Now I can. Esteban, what are you doing? Don't go out there, what are . . ."

"I'll be all right, and I'll be right back, Nieves."

"But, Esteban, you don't . . . here, take a lantern or something, don't rush off like that."

"Don't worry, Nieves . . . it's probably nothing."

"Nothing? Then why're you going out then?"

"They've stopped."

"Esteban, please."

"Nieves: we both know that the Buenrostros and the Leguizamóns have . . ."

"But what's that to us? That's their affair, Esteban . . . . Not yours, ours, *theirs*."

"We have land, Nieves, and we have it and a house on it, and we do so because the Buenrostros *gave* us this land . . . . Have you forgotten that already?"

"These lands are ours, Esteban. Legally ours."

"Legally . . . hmph. And who held them against the Leguizamóns and their wolf-packs?''

"Well . . . . . . the Vilches families . . . and, and, and the Tueros, and . . .''

"Those families are dead, Nieves . . . long dead.''

"All right, the Buenrostros helped . . .''

"Helped? They *held* the land; don Jesús and don Julián stood up to be counted when it mattered, when it was a matter of life or death. Yes. Look, just hand me that lantern you spoke of. There they go again; hear 'em?''

"Blessed be the name of . . .''

"Amen and hand me that Thirty-Thirty while you're at it.''

Two months later, don Julián Buenrostro learned the *matones's* identity; and he learned it from Esteban Echevarría who came calling early one morning at the Carmen Ranch. An all-day conversation and then on the next day, the 12th of July and don Julián's birthday, he crossed the Rio Grande into Mexican soil, just above the Klail City pumping station.

A month after that, and again through the offices of Esteban Echevarría, don Julián learned that Alejandro Leguizamón had hired the two Mexican nationals to kill don Jesús.

As had been told elsewhere and at another time and place, Alejandro Leguizamón was found with both his head and his brains fairly-well bashed in; early church-goers found his body near the fenced-in patio leading to the north entrance of the Sacred Heart Church.

"They's gonna be hell to pay around here, don Alejandro; them Buenrostros just ain't going to take to this with their hands in their pockets . . .''

"Señor Markham, you worry too much.''

"Could be, but I know Julián Buenrostro and he'll come after you.''

"Oh, I know he'll come, but he won't come running, will he?"

"No, maybe not, but he'll come, just the same. He's the kind."

Alejandro Leguizamón shook his head lightly and smiled at Choche Markham: "Don't worry about it."

"Well, Mr. Leguizamón, tell you what: I'm going on into town for a while and see what's up."

"No need to worry . . . ."

One can never be too careful or too cautious either, it seems. Alejandro Leguizamón didn't outlive don Jesús Buenrostro by much, and it happened this way:

Alejandro Leguizamón had made an arrangement with a woman; they were to meet after the Sacred Heart bazaar on a Sunday evening. But, and this is nothing new, instead of the woman, Alejandro Leguizamón found Julián Buenrostro waiting for him, tire iron in hand.

The Older Generation I

Don Marcial de Anda, a religious, pious soul, used to sell homemade candy under the palm grove at the corner of Klail and Cooke Boulevard. He's a small-boned, timid little man; and generous. *Un hombre de bien*, then. He's watching the occasional traffic on Klail Avenue as he sits on a city park bench donated by the Sons and Daughters of Some Revolution or Other. It's a bit warmish, but he is seventy-odd years old and anything under 85 °F is cold as far as he's concerned: A Valley Mexican, he is Belken-born and bred. He begins to roll a cigarette; looking up, he smiles as I approach. His eyes smile, too, and then a slight shake of the head.

"Peace," he says.

"And how are you today, don Marcial?"

"Fine, fine; just taking in the sun, Rafe."

"Can I join in?"

"Ho! Here, I'll just move over . . . . Tell me, Rafe, how are the Buenrostros getting along?"

"Fine, thanks; and you're looking well yourself."

"You in school, are you?"

"Yessir; up at Austin."

"Ah, yes . . . the univeristy. Good! Ha, did I ever tell you 'bout your Dad 'n me? Well, the first time I met him, I was about your age, and I worked for him a while later on. Well, worked *with* him is more like it; he was like that. A good man, your Dad."

"At El Carmen Ranch?"

"That's right; right by the river. I was a mule breaker. Ah . . . I was slightly older than he was . . . that puts me what? Four? Five years older'n your uncle Julián? That sounds right; I'll be seventy-five next winter. What do you think a-that? Seventy-five."

"Seventy-five . . . has it been a good life, don Marcial?"

"Oh, the best. Good land. Good people. Plenty of water. Ah, you want to know why I want to be seventy-five years old?"

Nod.

"It's the *idea* of it; three-quarters of a century. Something to shoot for. It's not the *number* of years; I mean, Jesus was crucified and died and rose at age thirty-three, but that don't make me two and a half times as good as the Lord; no sir. It's the *idea*, see? Three-quarters of a century. That's a long time in man-years."

"Hope you get another seventy-five, and I hope I get to see them." Repeating the age-old compliment.

"Ho, ho! No chance a-that, boy. You, ah, you barkeeping this summer?"

Nod.

"At Dirty's, right?"

"Summers, vacations . . . whenever."

"Never thought I'd see the day . . . *El quieto*'s boy tending bar . . . oh, don't take offense, son. Everyone's got to live his *own* life; no interference, no sir. I believe in Good God Almighty, but that don't mean I believe in the priests. Hmph. I played marbles with Pedro Zamudio as a child, and here he is, a mission priest. What does he know, I ask you? No, no criticism intended or meant on your part, son."

"And none taken, don Marcial. You've known me all my life."

"Good God's truth, and my wife delivered you herself, didn't she? Ha! Remember when you had that arm sprain a-yours? You was playing ball or something . . ."

"Fell off a tree." Smile.

"That's *right*. That chinaberry, out at the ranch . . . Well, I cured that, remember?"

"I sure do . . . I must've been fourteen then . . ."

"And your Dad'd just been buried, too."

"That's right . . ."

"You, ah, you remember that foreman your Dad had then? That foreman had a boy younger'n you . . . the kid couldn't walk; paralyzed. Kept him in a box, remember? Oh, I rubbed that boy, too, but . . . he died when you and your cousin were out in Korea."

He lights another hand rolled cigarette. "On your way to work, are you?"

Nod.

I sit listening to this fine old man. Good land, good people. Plenty of water . . . . And here I am, going to college. Shit; what do I know?"

A little background. Don Marcial de Anda is Jovita's father, and Jovita is the girl who had to marry Joaquín, the oldest of the Tamez brothers. Don Marcial is a grandfather; at first, he used to look after the kids; a babysitter. Now, the kids themselves are growing up, and *they* take care of him. They're at the park, too, running, yelling, playing, and every once in a while one of them comes over and asks him how he's doing, and then returns to play some more. Come supper, the kids'll walk him home, and don Marcial will sit on the east porch watching the kids, the grownups, and most of Texas Mexican Klail City stroll by.

But how is one to know what'll come next? It must be going on fifteen years now that old don Servando Tamez single-handedly arranged Joaquín's and Jovita's marriage, and again, at don Servando's insistence, that no de Andas were to be present. And now, rains have come and gone, crops raised and people buried (and don Servando along with them) and even gimpy Emilio Tamez married off: a Monroy girl who turned out to be more than a match for him, too. As for Bertita Tamez, well, she did elope and marry a hardworking kid, Ramiro Leal, who put his economic mark in Muleshoe (West Texas). The oldest boy, Joaquín, married Jovita, of course, and then Ernesto, the youngest, was killed at the *Aquí me quedo*; stabbed to death by Balde Cordero, a most unlikely killer, by the way. Still, it must be said that Ernesto himself provoked his own death; it happens.

Yes, and how *is* one to tell what'll happen next? Take the Tamez family: rowdy and tough; the de Andas, mild and meek; Emilio married to a Monroy, Bertita to a Leal; don Servando and Ernesto eating dirt at the mexicano cemetery in Bascom, and there's don Marcial on the porch rocking-chair in his own daughter's house; 'cause that's whose house it is now. A peaceful occupying army, the de Andas. A house, known to all, where he wasn't welcomed, but that's all changed, mutatis mutandis. He has his own room, his chocolate with cinnamon, and his house slippers under that old, handmade, four-poster pecan wood bed which belonged to his wife, the late Lorenza Estudillo de Anda.

So, who knows what'll happen next? Specters and visions, voices and sounds, all stuck and nailed and caught in the walls of the Tamez house:

"Jovita! That door there leads to my wife's room; Joaquín was born there and so were Emilio and Bertie-Babe. My wife died there, too. You go in there and sit on the bed, and don't open the door until I say so."

"Couldn't wait, could you? Just had to pull 'em down, didn't you? And now what? This! Good God Almighty, Joaquín . . ."

"Ernesto, don't you be stopping anywhere along the way. You got that? I want you back here before three o'clock . . . move it!"

"Listen, Joaquín, this house and everything in it is all we got, but it's ours. And when I die, you'll be in charge. In charge, Joaquín."

And that was it. In time, Joaquín took charge of the running of the family on don Servando's death; fate was kind, though, and don Servando did get to hug and kiss two of his five grandchildren. (Jovita won out, of course; the first child, Tulita, was named for her deceased mother-in-law.) The other four were named for don Marcial de Anda and for his three sons. The Tamezes? Shut out, with no hits, no runs, etc.

"You doing all right, Dad?"

"Oh, yes. Thank you." Smile.

"Sleep well, did you?"

"Like a top; and you, Jovita?"

"Like a baby (giggle) . . . . Would you like your chocolate now?"

The three bachelor de Anda brothers belong to the Nativity of our Blessed Lady Church parish. Serious, industrious, they branched out their father's homemade candy business; they're in their forties and each one—every day—after mass, calls on don Marcial at the park; the talk is about this and that; nothing new, and the routine's the same, too. And so, later on of an evening, the bachelors (*los cotorrones*, what we call bachelors here) march off to that small house of theirs on the lots my father gave them years ago.

Ten o'clock, and I'm on my way home from work at the *Aquí me quedo*; the kerosene lamplight is on in don Marcial's room. The house is wired, of course, but he prefers a lamp. Why not? One thing's for sure: he's reading a bible my cousin Jehu gave him a few years back . . . . The porch is in darkness, but I can make out the two shapes in the rocking chairs:

"A good evening, Rafe Buenrostro."

"And a good one to the both of you."

"Things well at home? Family all right?"

"Yes, thanks, Jovita. I'll tell my brothers you asked."

"Night."

"Night."

Tomorrow, and if God cooperates, don Marcial, one day behind and another one coming up, will take himself to the park again and wait for the winter which will mark his seventy-fifth year in Klail City, Belken County.

"Don Marcial; are we doing all right?"

"Enjoying God's own sun, Rafe . . . . And you?"

The Older Generation II

Don Aureliano Mora is one tough old man, and I'm leaving damn little room for argument here. Time's gotten to him some, but he's neither down for the count nor out of circulation. His eyesight's down a peg, but that's about it for this tough, wiry old man.

He's eighty-two years old, and, as he says: ". . . and I can still dress myself, thank you." According to him, only three types need help getting dressed: newborns, madmen, and all the Popes of Rome. I nod as I listen to this fine old man and remember he's buried five of his seven sons and daughters; he has one living dau., Obdulia, married to one of the Santoscoy boys, and Eufrasio, who's got a touch of T.B. He's had it for thirty years.

Don Aureliano is—was—the father to Ambrosio Mora, a World War II vet shot and killed by Belken County Deputy Sheriff Van Meers right in front of Klail's J.C. Penney Store on a Palm Sunday, as the song says.

Young Mora had been an infantryman in the Second Division (Indianhead) during the French invasion; and, he stood a mere thirty feet away from Chano Ortega, another Klail City youngster, who died during the drive for the Cerisy Forest on D-Day plus two. Young Mora and Ortega were among the numerous Texas mexicanos who'd volunteered for army service a year before this country declared war on the so-called Axis Powers.

On a Palm Sunday (in Flora town)

Ambrosio Mora's murder brought about a change; gradually, but a change. Something. The old men didn't know how to go about making a change, but they *knew* something had to give. They looked to the veterans: yes! This shit's got-to-stop, some of them said.

Sure. But what? A lot of talk and a lot of noise, but first, what with one thing and then another followed by those-oh-so-familiar trial delays, interest began to peter out. The result? Well, the trial came up three years later, and Deputy Sheriff Van Meers walked right out of that court house over there. Free as a bird shitting on the house roofs. (Ranger George Markham and not as a by the way (by the way), spoke in Van Meers's defense. Oh, yes.)

This was 1949, a year before Korea, and the mexicano people *again* raised some hell, but no, nothing came of it until don Aureliano Mora himself took matters (in the shape of a crowbar) into his own hands.

He got himself a crowbar and marched to the old Klail City Park, stood in front of a metal plaque (a County Historical Marker, they called it), and standing there, reading the names of those who fought and some of whom had died in World War II (Young Ambrosio Mora's name was there as was that of Amador Mora who died alongside Ernie Pyle in Okinawa), don Aureliano rested his eyes on the two Mora names and WHANG! he broke that plaque in half; he then proceeded to smash and shatter the damn thing into very small pieces. After this, he ground the pieces into the Bermuda grass; not saying a word. He looked around the park that hot afternoon: no witnesses. It doesn't matter, he humphed.

That plaque had been a loving gift from the Ladies' Auxiliary of the American Legion, and the old man had been taken to its dedication by his daughter Obdulia a few years before.

Once finished, don Aureliano, bar in hand, went to see don Manuel Guzmán.

A coward, gun in hand (gunned Young Mora down)

"Don Manuel, I just got back from the park; remember the War Plaque? . . . Well, I just got done breaking the living hell and memory a-the damn thing."

No heat in the voice.

And then: "Here's the crowbar."

Don Manuel Guzmán took the Bull Durham cigarette from his mouth, looked at it, and then at his old friend:

"Keep it; you might need it for work, later on."

"I, ah, I not only broke it, I smashed it, ground it down, see? But what *could* I do? They killed my boy, don Manuel . . . . I waited three years, don Manuel . . . and then to see that smiling, banjo-faced, big-footed, ham-eating, red-necked sanna-va-bitchy go free? Well! Here I am, I'll take my medicine."

"Josefa! Bring don Aureliano a glass of limeade. Be right back, gonna put my shoes on."

Don Manuel took don Aureliano home; there'll be no jail for this old man, he said.

"We're Greeks, don Manuel. Greeks . . . Greeks whose homes have been taken over by the Romans."

Don Manuel took a right turn, shifted his old Chevy up to second, and looked at don Aureliano: "You, ah, you want to run that one by again?"

"We're like the Greeks, don Manuel. Slaves in service of the Romans . . . . we've got to educate them, these Romans, these Anglos . . . amounts to the same thing."

Nod from don Manuel. "Well, I'll tell you what, don Aureliano: Only God can make things perfect, and in this case, He made some perfect sansa-bitches. Am I right, or what? . . . But, it all comes out in the wash . . ."

"And we'll all be dried on the line," finished don Aureliano Mora.

"As for that *sign*, that plaque, or whatever, I'll handle that end of it . . ."

"But what if . . ."

"No. No *what ifs*. We'll hire a lawyer, if it comes to that. Yessir . . . and I'd like to see them make a case about the destruction of public property. Hmph! They'll be talking about a piece of metal, and we'll talk about a man, a veteran; a kid of twenty-three, for Christ's sakes."

Nod from don Aureliano. "Greeks, yeah; but the day'll come when we'll see this ground as ours again. As sure as there's a God somewhere around here."

The park incident took place twenty-two years ago, and don Aureliano's Greeks didn't educate the Romans, but they did educate themselves in the ways of the Romans; some even turned out the same way. But they were Greeks for all that, and the proof is in the taste, not in the pudding, as we say.

So Young Mora was shot in the back. What a cowardly act!

Don Aureliano Mora has moved to a shady part of the park; he's sitting in one of the six benches that are left now. Thinking, perhaps, of Amador who died in Okinawa; on Serafín who left and never returned to Belken County: Serafín gave thirty years of his life to Inland Steel; in return, the company gave him a pension, and then, at his death, the Social Security Administration threw in a coffin; on the twins, Antonio and Julio who lived and worked and died; and surely, on

Ambrosio, the Flower of the Flock, on whose behalf a *co-rrido*, a ballad, was written and sung, and for whom don Aureliano decided to rid Belken County of still another piece of cold hypocrisy that served as a slap in the face of that old man.

Once in a while, the old man gets up and walks to the east corner of the park. A smile. No; no more plaques; a clothing store now. (One mustn't stand in the way of progress). The park, named for General Rufus T. Klail, has been subdivided and sold into lots; a mini mall, they call it, and this is where the Romans sell their wares and souls on a daily basis. What's left of the park is a strip of six benches, and that's where the old man spends most of his days.

He'll die, of course; it's only a matter of time, after all. Don Aureliano smiles: he's made a pact with God, no less. He's not to take don Aureliano until Van Meers dies. Don Aureliano's got over twenty-five years on the Deputy, but don Aureliano says he's got something else on his side: patience. Oh, yes; and, confidence enough to know he'll be a witness to Van Meers' funeral.

"Don Aureliano, you doing all right?"

"Doing just fine, son. Whose boy are you?"

"My name's Rafe Buenrostro."

"Of course! Don Jesús's boy . . . *el quieto*; you're Quieto Junior. A good man, your father. A fine man. You're a University man, I hear . . . That's good." Nod. "Good."

As a shield against the fierce Belken County sun, don Aureliano wears one of those *sombreros de petate*, the broad-brimmed, stiff straw hat. He looks at me: "It's coffee time, Young Buenrostro."

He gets up without any help from me, and we walk across the street to Maggie Guevara's Cupboard. It doesn't seem as if don Aureliano steps on the grass when he walks; a light step and one would think that a stiff Gulf breeze would blow the man down. But, as Gómez Manrique said in those *coplas* of his: "No, no se equivoque nadie, no . . ." The man's not about to be blown away; not yet.

Appearances *can* be deceiving, and I'm putting my money on this old horse; he'll bury Van Meers, all right, and I'm taking bets.

The Older Generation III

April 11, 1920
Klail City, Tex.

My dear Manuel:

Just a few lines to let you know we're doing well here despite the flu epidemic. Other than a runny nose here and there, the kids and I are bearing up. No need to worry on your account.

> "Sergeant Buitrón says to remount; let's go, now."
> "Yeah? Well, you can tell that crazy son-of-a-bitch . . ."

The one piece of bad news is that Spanish influenza. It's covered both sides of the Río Grande now. We're still at the ranch, and it looks as if it's staying in the town, not out here. We're fine. Okay?

The Lambs of God blame the epidemic on past sins, on the Revolution, on our own inherent badness, but you know how that goes. The danger of all this is that some sharper is going to come along and take the people for a bath selling them candles, rosaries, incense—anything to strip them off what money the poor are holding on to.

"Well? What are you going to do? Quit? Want me to go back to Sergeant Buitrón and tell him that?"

"Remigio, we know you're dumb, you don't have to keep proving it, you know. You've got your corporal's stripes now, so shut up."

"Don't you guys hear that gunfire over there? Get the horses!"

"Get your mother!"

"That's right; why isn't that troop over there going on the charge?"

"He told me to tell you, not them."

"Up yours."

"Manuel! Come on . . . talk to these guys, will you?"

Dr. Webber is the only doctor in Klail City now. We'll make out all right. We have before, you know. I've already advised the folk to spray gasoline to burn up the stagnant water holes. I pointed out to them that it's the mosquitoes we've got to kill. I've already sent Amadeo to Relámpago to pick up the old folks. He's to bring your mother here, with us. Amadeo's grown and he looks so much like you. He'll be as tall as you, if not taller.

"Ha! Does Buitrón know how many horses we got left in the troop? Well? We're not even at half-strength, Remigio. We're ten out of twenty-five. Shit! Look at Cruz over there; the Red Cross guy says he hasn't got a chance . . ."

"Please, Manuel . . . talk to 'em, will you? They'll listen to you. Tell 'em to mount up."

Two Midwest Anglos came by last week. Again. It's the

same old story: they want to gobble up more of the land. For developing, they call it. They say they want it for agriculture and for fruit trees. I told them they'd have to wait until your return. I doubt you know either one. The slim one learned to use Spanish somewhat, and he'll probably use this to overcome some mexicano resistance. His partner's a red-headed, freckled-faced dwarf. All *he* does is smile.

"Way to go, boys! That's the stuff men are made of, yessir. We showed them a thing or two, right?

"Remigio, why don't you just shut the hell up?"

"Yeah. Where were you when we went after that train? I sure as hell didn't see you here."

"I was there, you just didn't see me, that's all."

"Bullshit. None of us saw you."

"I was there, I tell you."

"Leave him alone; go on, Remigio, get out of here."

"Manuel! Ah . . . Báez just died."

"Yeah, Manuel, the Red Cross guy even brought a surgeon 'n everything."

"Yeah, well someone go tell Remigio we're down to five men."

"Oh, he knows. It's six, counting him. Hmph."

"Manuel, you notice how some of the train guys threw their rifles out?"

"Yeah . . . they're probably just as tired of this as we are."

What with the flu epidemic and the people staying away from the fields, it doesn't look as if we'll have much of a cotton crop this season. Here we are, two weeks into April and the bolls are barely out. It's hot enough, but without the weeding to cut down the growth—I don't mean to burden you with this, and I won't. We'll make it, we always have.

Don't worry about us. I mean it. I miss you, and I love you, and God willing you'll soon be reading this. I'll mail it from Matamoros. I'll cross the river tonight and see if this gets to you sooner that way. Speaking of Matamoros, Alvaro Obregón is politicking up in this neck of the woods.

Your loving wife,

Josefa

"All right, now. What's the count?"

"Eight dead, six wounded, and ten missing."

"Missing? You mean *deserted*, don't you?"

"I . . . I . . . don't know."

"Well, hell, I can't blame 'em . . . Go call Manuel Guzmán over here."

"Him? What for?"

"Remigio, *that* is none of your god-damned business."

"Ah . . . ah . . ."

"Move!"

"*Yes*sir."

Sergeant Leonides Buitrón looked at the return address: PO Box 245, Klail City, Texas, U.S.A. He handed the letter to Pvt. Manuel Guzmán on May 10, 1920, at Aljibes, Puebla.

Guzmán, an American citizen as his father and his father's father before him, formed part of a cavalry troop chasing President Venustiano Carranza's trains on their way to Veracruz. This detachment was led by General Sánchez, an Obregón backer.

It was Obregón, by the way, who later recommended Manuel Guzmán for the post of chief jailer at Lecumberri Prison in 1921.

The Searchers

Another bone-dry summer in Belken County. The cotton's about played out, and there's been no rain to count on since last March. The Gulf breeze pushes its hot wind through the wooden fence; everything's on fire, it seems. There *is* one spot of a cool breeze, and that's under the chinaberry trees; but that's about it. The drought hangs on like a feisty dog on a rat . . .

Some Women

"And the kids?"

"A little better, thanks. Annie, too."

"It never stops, does it?"

"Ah-ha; if it isn't this, it's something else or worse."

"Isn't that the truth? And Dorothea; how is *she*? Have you heard?"

"Oh, yes; ran away, they say."

"Again?"

"Oh, yeah: again . . ."

"Who with this time? Not that same boy again, is it?"

"Seems as if she was carrying on with Ernesto Tamez, and . . ."

"Really? Oh, she picked herself a peck of trouble this time . . ."

"You didn't know about that?"

"About the Tamez boy? No, I'd heard it was one of the Murillo kids."

"Oh, that's old news."

"And the youngest Murillo?"

"Up North, I imagine . . . so Dorothea Amejorado went and did it . . . . And how's that brother of hers? Balta? Weren't they after him to have his tonsils out?"

"That's what the school nurse told Señor Amejorado."

"Hmph. As my Fabián says: Next to God, you've got to hand it to the Anglos; they keep coming up with a disease every week."

"Isn't that God's truth? Ah, but this heat: I don't think I've seen anything like it before; when was the last time it rained around here?"

"You know, old man Sobrino says this reminds him of a similar drought fifty years ago . . . . . Kheeww."

"And the Relámpago folks? Hear anything from them out there?"

"Getting older, I guess."

"Aren't we all, comadre . . . Come on, let's go back inside for a minute; we've got some nice ice cold limeade."

"Oh, that *would* be nice; we'll have the glass, but then we've *got* to be going; one of the kids has been acting up. Upset stomach, you know."

"Remind me to pass you some balm gentle before you do leave; and then, later this evening, we'll drop by and I'll bring her some lettuce-leaf tea. That'll settle her tummy."

"That *is* nice, comadre."

Their husbands

"And again no rain today . . . it's a bad sign when the weeds themselves are so puny."

"What about Molonco Ramírez? How's he doing?"

"Same as us, I guess. You haven't heard from him, then?"

"Not for a month or so; I got that irrigator of his to working again, though."

"Hmmm. He need something fixed, he'll come by again." (Laugh)

"Ah, he's not such a bad guy."

"I know that . . . . You, ah, you got your two boys working somewhere?"

"No trouble. Those two hustle *all* the time; took 'em to the races last Sunday."

"Horses? This time a-year?"

"No; a car race . . . it's not really a race. They crash 'em into each other."

"Crash 'em? On purpose?"

"Yeah . . . what do you think about that?"

"Those Texas Anglos take the cake, the candles and the icing."

"Speaking of *them*, there's talk of them fixing the streets again . . ."

"Sure they are; come election time we'll hear that one again."

"God's truth, but some people are willing to believe anything you tell 'em."

"Ye-know, it's a bit early, but a couple of trucks headed Up North last week. I worked on the cab and the rigging on both of them; spot cash."

"You got paid in cash?"

"Oh, yeah."

"I remember you worked on Leocadio Gavira's truck . . . who that second one belong to?"

"Kara-mel and Jake went halves on it."

"Those two are in-laws, right? . . . Hmmm. I wonder how things are Up North?"

"Fine, according to them; we're all going to have start thinking about another trip, compadre."

"Hmph . . . well, looks like the women are through over there."

"Why don't you all just come on over tonight. Visit a while."

"That sounds pretty good."

"Where's that funny race track you were talking about?"

"Oh, that . . . out to Edgerton, by the west side stock yards."

"Hmmm, I'll see if I can take my kids out there next Friday."

"You'll like it; craziest thing I've ever seen . . . ."

Straw hats, khaki shirts and pants; house slippers and colored house dresses. Brown hands and faces. Strong teeth, chins, eyes, noses. One season blends with the next and one type of work doesn't differ from any other. Ever.

The Searchers II

Indiana bound! The Del Monte Company's hiring from Indiana! All expenses paid, folks! And there's an advance too! Listen to this: there's a partial payment for the way *up* and then a partial for the way *back*. Guaranteed! Whatta-ya-say? And! Yes! We're paying time-and-a-half for any time over fifty-five hours a week. Indiana! Indiana bound!

It's August in Belken County, and the cotton pickings are slim since the third pick's been done with. The citrus crop (and it's looking good) is still some four months away; December the earliest. The citrus season will then last till March provided it doesn't freeze over in Dec. or Jan. or Feb. With any luck at all, there *could* be a remnant citrus crop in April, but this is too much to hope for. So, there's nothing to do but go Up North. Take one's chances on the road up and back, 1500 mi., each way. A bitch.

"Well? Shall we sign up with Mad Mike and go on up to Indiana this year?"

"We got another choice?"

"Sure. We can stay here and eat shit till December."

"Ah, hell; Indiana ain't so bad. Let's sign up with him."

"How 'bout you all, what do you plan to do?"

"The way we got it figured, we can make it from Klail to Texarkana in about fourteen hours. Then, we cut across Arkansas and on up to Poplar Bluff, in Missouri, and then to Kankakee. Well'p, once in Kankakee, Illinois, we can head for Monon, Indiana or Reynolds or maybe even Kentland; there's bound to be work in some of those places."

"And you all?"

"Well, we might just go up to Texarkana way, too . . . the trouble is that Arkansas has terrible roads."

"Well, I heard they'd been fixed over."

"Hmph . . . that's something we hear every year and then what happens when we get there? . . . . There we go, barreling down those bad roads like cows down a chute . . . But what the hell, Indiana and Illinois both got bad, poor, narrow, no shoulder roads . . ."

"That's true, but listen to this: I heard Arkansas's come through: they got themselves a wide road that cuts clear across the state. As good as Texas roads, I hear."

"Made just for *us*, right? Shoot . . . we got mighty fine roads in Texas, all right, but this here state a-ours is a skinflintish son-of-a-bitch."

"Amen!"

"Michigan! I say, Michigan! Who's for Michigan? Folks, listen to me: Big Buddy Cucumber—la pepinera—guarantees the trip for you, your wife, *and* family. Yes! Big Buddy! And, we got cement floor cabins, a tile roof, electricity, running water, name it . . . Who'll sign on for Michigan? This way . . ."

"Aniceto, don't forget to board up the windows really good, now."

"Don't worry . . . just keep the kids in the shade, okay?"

"Up North! Up North! Leocadio Gavira pays for *everything*! A promise given is a promise kept! That's the Gavira guarantee. And looky here: we further promise to have you back in Belken County by December . . . or earlier. Yes! A promise! Be back in time for orange-picking time. Whadda-ya-say?"

"Who you leaving your house keys with this year?"

"That's an easy one: Don Manuel Guzmán, who else?"

"And what about the kids' schooling?"

"Well, it's not on yet, a-course, being summer time and all, but we'll enroll them in Indiana, and then, when we get back to Klail in December, we'll enroll 'em again . . . ."

"The girls should be finishing up the sun-bonnets by now; remind them of the ear flaps, while you're at it. It gets cold early up there."

"God's truth."

"And you all?"

"Pete Leyva . . . he's our man."

"That's right . . . he's fair, but you still got to watch him."

"Aw, we'll watch him. We'll make out."

"Oh, I don't mean to run old Pete down; he does what he can, and he knows the way. Stops at safe places, too."

"That's true."

"And how about you all?"

"No. We're going with Leocadio Gavira."

"*The Oklahoma Fireball Express* himself, yessir."

"That's the one for us, too."

"You bet!"

"It's 'cause we know him, see?"

"Need a helper! A good one! An English-speaking helper and driver's assistant! Good pay, room *and* board! Any volunteers? You got to have a license, though . . . and . . . and, the pay's good, too."

"The Cardonas would like to borrow the hammer, Dad."

"Sure thing; ask 'em if they need some nails."

"Kids! Kids! Out of the way, now; and out of the sun, too. Come on, out to the shade, now."

"Look, you have got to take care of yourself. The understanding, the contract; okay? That's done *here*, in the Valley, not up *there*, in the North."

"That's what I say."

"Same here . . ."

"Damn right. And you *got* to watch them, otherwise they'll keep you up there till January or February, even. That's right."

"Remember what happened *last* year?"

"Ha! Look, December, and that's the latest. Come December, and that's *it*, back to Klail."

"Hear, hear."

"And your family?"

"Don't know yet . . . . We may sign up with the Del Monte Company, but I don't know if we're going on to Indiana or Michigan . . . we're still talking."

"How about Ohio, then?"

"Maybe, and maybe not."

And you?

The Searchers III

"Pleased to meet you, Mr. Galindo. I'd *heard* of you, of course, but I'd never had the pleasure. How you doing?"

"Fine; thank you. And you?" Smile.

"Well, don Manuel Guzmán, he filled me in on you, your plan?"

"Yes."

"So, if there's anything—*anything* I can do, just say the word."

"That's very kind of you, but it's pretty straight forward: I'd like to make the trip Up North with you. In your truck."

"Oh, is that it? Sure thing. Nothing to it."

"Not too much to ask, is it?"

"No sir; you're as welcome as rain. Anytime."

"Tomorrow morning then?"

"Four thirty, right before sun break, Mr. Galindo. We'll be all set to go by then; we pull out of Almanza's filling station, and we won't look back. How's that?"

"I appreciate it, Mr. Gavira."

"No bother; any friend of don Manuel's is a friend of mine. Yes sir."

P. Galindo, a Klail City native, was twenty-eight at the time of this conversation; he's thirty-six now, and Time, the great leveler, has taken care of some of the people in the upcoming narrative. Some have gone off, others are still hanging in there, and still others have blended into the woodwork. So to speak.

The writer—this writer—when he was a child, believed as a child. Believed, then, with little proof but with all his heart. There's a bit of the child in him still, but he prefers the truth, above all.

What follows, then, in some readable, reasonable order, started off as notes for something called *One Mexican's Michigan*. The title was changed and finally dropped altogether. A new start produced the inevitable changes again, but *Klail City* presented itself as a title; it was both brief and to the point.

The trips with Señor Gavira were made in good faith, and the writer managed to pull his load. He changed any number of flat tires, and he spelled the two drivers on occasion; most importantly, he got out of everyone's way when it was necessary he do so.

To add to this, the writer wanted to remember certain people and make sure that these people were remembered in writing. The writer is convinced that he did well not to have written about the trips on the spot; he believes in Time, that leveler he spoke of.

The writer worked in some very odd jobs and for some very odd people for the first thirty years of his life. Some of those people may be dead by now, but as we say, dying comes the once, but it comes for all. In the course of that time, schooling of all forms and shapes interfered as well, as did some personal events. Time has convinced him that none of those events are of particular or peculiar interest to anyone. This now includes the writer himself.

The trips with Leocadio Gavira are akin to the reconstruction of an old house that needs saving, holding on to; one begins with a bit of work here and there, a bit of retouching, and all done carefully, lovingly almost. What follows is merely the first day's drive northward, and the writer considers this trip as something of an important pilgrimage to him and to the working people on the migrant trails.

Those odd jobs and those odder people referred to earlier caused the writer to change his style of life for a while, but this proved to be temporary. But, it was also beneficial: the writer needed that experience too, after all. The writer now feels he's back on track, having recovered, ransomed perhaps, the knowledge of who he was and where he came from. Time and Life, both, had erased some of that self-knowledge, but the writer—if he is nothing else—thinks himself quite lucky and fortunate, too, to have recovered a part of his life that he'd almost forgotten, that he had, insensibly, unthinkingly, turned his back on, temporarily.

"Actually, it-a, it was already a used-truck when I bought it off Paulino Saucedo; you know him?"

"Oh, sure; a nice guy."

"You all must be around the same age; am I right?"

"Just about . . . I'd say he's three, maybe four years older than I am; no more 'n that, though."

"Hmmmm. See that little wire-thing there, on the glove box?"

"Right there?"

"Right. Pull it toward you just a bit and see if that'll open it. There! Now, there should be some pictures there . . . you find 'em?"

"Right here; here's one of you, and, here's one of Paulino himself. Who's that with you all? A skinny guy, curly hair . . ."

"Well now, that must be Víctor Jara, the Caramel Kid . . . . You, ah, you couldn't make him out, eh? Is there anything written on the back, like a date or something?"

"Yeah; it's in pencil: P. Saucedo, Leocadio G., and let's see: KARA-MEL, with a *K* and a dash."

"Yeah, that's 'cause he's a character."

"Funny guy . . ."

"Funny and a half. You sure you don't know him? He's from Edgerton originally, but he married a Klail girl."

"Oh, I might have seen him, but I don't know him to talk to."

"Oh, well, you know him by sight then, and that's enough."

"Hard to tell what people are like from the outside, I mean."

"That's true, too, Señor Galindo. Right as rain, yessir. Can't tell by the looks of a watermelon either, can you? That reminds me of something that happened to Kara-Mel over to Princeville, Illinois. You been there?"

"No. Whereabouts is it?"

"Those Marathon Oil maps place it just south of Peoria, but I'd say it's probably closer to Hell'n anything else."

Laugh from P. Galindo. "Is there a story?"

"Yeah, like what you were saying just now: can't tell by appearances and all that. The people in that there place looked nice, but damned if they were . . . . Hooo."

"Pretty bad?"

"Oh, yeah; I'll tell you about that town some day; I'll tell you what happened to a truck load of us there one picking season."

"Anytime's fine with me; I'm here for company."

"And I appreciate it, yes*sir*. I usually hire someone to help me out here, drive a bit, . . . a kid who speaks English, don't you know. You ever drive a truck, Señor Galindo?"

"No. Much different from a car, is it?"

"We—ll, a truck's heavier, for one, but you know that. What I meant was that there's the people back there to think about: women, kids, and you got to be careful. Considerate, too. Keep an eagle eye out for curves, bad shoulders, rain-slicked highways, and like that."

"And a kid, a teenager, say fifteen or so, he can handle a truck like this one?"

"Not all of 'em, that's the truth, but once in a while, you get hold of one of those good ones, like they was born to the road; know what I mean?"

"A natural."

"That's *right*, a natural."

"Yeah, but now, you've got me."

"And don't forget Balta Amejorado up in the back . . . but you look like you could sit right behind the wheel there . . . you look the type."

Laugh. "Cause I'm skin and bone?"

"Ha! That's a good one, but you're right; skinny folks are pretty tough, as a rule. Really; I'm not just saying that; yeah, I can spot talent; got to."

"Well, Mr. Gavira, just say the word, but I do have to tell you that I don't have a commercial license."

"Oh, that's okay, but I appreciate the offer, and I'll take you up on it. It's a long haul up to Michigan.

"Now, the first big town we hit in Texas is Houston; I'll probably let you take over for an hour or so. And then, when we get to Arkansas, but that's hours away, I can let you take over again; the cops ain't as picky there, see? When we cut into Missouri, you can drive some more there. We don't stay long in Missouri though, and we'll be in Illinois before you know it. But, we'll stop in Missouri on the second night; we'll check the tires and the lights . . . it's a regular place for us. They know us there . . . ." Nod to P. Galindo.

"So we won't be too long there, in Missouri?"

"A couple of hours and then we bed down."

"Do we cross at Cairo, Illinois?"

"That's right. You been there, have you?"

"Yes. But on the Kentucky side."

"Aha . . . I don't know that region; how is it there?"

"Something like East Texas; a lot of trees, water . . . I spent couple of cotton seasons in Memphis, sometime back."

"Oh, Señor Galindo, I've been to Memphis, Tennessee and East Memphis, Arkansas . . . but, what was the Kentucky trip?"

"Oh, that was something else."

"I see . . . I, ah, I didn't mean to pry."

A shake of the head. "Nothing to it; a government job and some trouble with the labor contractors."

"Yeah. You got to watch 'em like hawks. Hmph. Don Manuel said you was in the service at one time."

"Yeah. That too was something else."

"Yeah? Did you know Amadeo Guzmán? Don Manuel's boy that was killed out in the Pacific"

"No. I knew who he was, sure. He was some five years older, I think."

"Hmmmmm. Ah, you want to look in the pictures there again? There's some in color."

"Here's Kara-Mel again. A woman; she Anglo?"

"Yep; she's the wife to the man who runs the country store in Sikeston, Missouri; right nice woman, too. Bob's Place; that's where we stop for over night; and we load up on saltines, cold cuts, Velveeta, Coca-Colas . . . about a mile a-fore you get there, there's a R C Cola sign and it says: Willcome to Our Mexican Friends." Gavira smiles.

"Willcome?"

"Aha, misspelled, right? That's what I told 'em. Anyway, we stop there; been stopping there for years; I'd say fifteen to twenty; this here truck is the sixth Oklahoma Fireball Express I got . . .

"Now, Jehu Malacara took those photographs. He was my chief helper that season; a good kid. Sharp, too. Been in the Army, like you. He's gone up to the University, up to Austin. You know him?"

"Sure; he's a Relámpago boy."

Laugh from Gavira. "He sure is; I like him."

"He's Rafe Buenrostro's age, just about."

"Buenrostro. Is that Julián's boy, Mr. Galindo?"

"No, you're thinking of Melchor. Rafe is—was—don Jesús's middle son . . ."

"Sure! What was I thinking about? He's *El quieto*'s boy; now there was a *señor*, that don Jesús."

"And you knew him, Señor Gavira?"

"No, not well; but I dealt with him a couple of times. Straight shooter. And you, Señor Galindo? Did you know him?"

"No. Knew of him, of course. I *do* know don Julián."

"And so do I. Yeah, he's no pushover either . . . . That man's got 'em hanging right in place, yessir. They're made a-brass, as we say . . . . He's up in years, now . . . . . . well . . . so am I. And you Señor Galindo, how old are you?"

"Twenty-eight."

"Hmmm. Me, I couldn't hit sixty with a shotgun."

"You're over sixty, Mr. Gavira? I pegged you at fifty-five, top."

"That's what everybody says." Laughing. Grinning. "But I know better. Come some of those early morning Valley fogs out-a that Gulf of Mexico, oh my, do I feel the years . . . . Ah, back to the photograph, the woman's name is Numa Zena, but we call her *Gumersinda*; that's the closest thing to Numa Zena . . . a strange name that."

"Sounds like one of those black names."

"Don't it, though. But she ain't. You got the picture in your hand. Aw, she ain't much to look at, but she's good people, know what I mean?"

"Sure do . . . and that's what counts."

"I'll say . . . but you've been on this route before, right?"

"Not for years; been a long time since I was up in Michigan."

"You work there, Señor Galindo?"

"Some . . ."

"Well, according to don Manuel Guzmán, you been working since you was a kid; he said you'd been up to Traverse City, Big Rapids, Reed City . . ."

"I did, when I was a kid."

"Who did your folks travel with on those trips?"

"We used to travel with the Cordero family."

"You . . . ah. You an orphan then?"

"Yes. My folks died in a train-truck accident years ago."

"The Flora wreck. Is that the one?"

"The very one . . ."

"Why, you must know Beto Castañeda."

"Oh, sure, we're cousins. I've got close to eight years on him."

"Well, since you mentioned the Corderos, I hit on Beto . . . good, hardworking kid. Useful and bright, too. No, he don't talk much, but he's no quitter, and I'm not just saying this 'cause you all are related, either. He really is a good one. Speaks English, too, and he *does* know them highways, all right. And work? Hooo. He, ah, he's sweet on Marta Cordero. He and Balde, that's Marta's brother, well, the two really get along. The Corderos raised Beto, you know that. Anyway, they're too young to think about marriage, but he and Marta make a nice couple . . ."

"I know the Corderos well, I first met don Albino up in Iowa."

"Mason City, right? Yeah . . . I usually sign 'em up or recommend them, one. Don Albino is a good man, no two ways about it. Brought up Balde the same way. My guess is that they're still back in the Valley; Klail. No idea who they're traveling with this year. Or where, either . . . Just so they don't sign up with Fat Frank Alvarado; he's a bad one, he is . . . .

"You notice that highway marker, Señor Galindo?"

"How's that again? I must've missed something."

"I said we'd be pulling into Rosenberg, Texas, in half an hour, soon as we're out of the city limits, you can spell me a bit. Okay with you?"

"Sounds good; looking forward to it."

"It's like I said, Señor Galindo: the years are catching up with me. All I need is a two-hour sleep, though, and I'll be good as new in no time . . . . Ha! Maybe not as good as new, no, but as good as the truck. Used, but in good condition, right?" Laugh.

"I'm here to help, Mr. Gavira. Just say the word, and I'll scoot on over."

Leocadio Gavira, owner and sole proprietor of the Dodge truck he baptized the *Oklahoma Fireball Express* stopped along the side of the road so I could take over. Some of the workers got off, wanting to know if there was something they could do to help, but Gavira explained that there was nothing to worry about.

"Change of driver is all. This here is Rosenberg, Texas; I'll sleep for a couple-a hours. Señor Galindo is a *good* driver. Now, if some of you have to go, *go* now."

Gavira got back into the cab and pointed the way for me.

"There's a public park four blocks down; we can take a pee break there. They all need to stretch out some, anyway."

The Okla. Fireball was half way to Texarkana that first day; the people, *la gente*, were all from Belken county—Klail City, Bascom, Flora, and Edgerton—and on their way to Benton Harbor and St. Joseph to work the Welch grape vineyards near Lake Michigan.

The Searchers IV

"Who's knocking down there? What do you want?"

"We need some help, some information . . . You the phar-macist"?

"Yeah; I'll be right down."

"Who is it, John?"

"Mexicans, I think."

"Are they sick or what?"

"Now, how in the world am I supposed to know that?"

"Keep your voice down, John."

"Oh, Christ . . . Where's the other shoe?"

"There, by the dresser. What time is it anyway?"

"Look at the nightstand there, four in the morning. Hey, down there. I'll be right down."

"I'm hungry."

"Same here, but first things first . . . We'll see."

"What are we down to?"

"Let's see . . . gas and the twenty I gave to that justice a-the peace . . . We got eleven left. Eleven dollars on the nose."

"Yeah, and now *this*."

"Don't worry about it. We got-a tank full of gas, there's enought for another tankful, and we got the two loaves of bread for the trip."

"Okay, folks, what's this all about?"

"My name is Rivas, and this is my wife. We're here about the two bodies in the wreck."

"Are you the son-in-law? The one who sent the telegram?"

"Yes, and I might's well tell you right off: I got eleven dollars and I need all but two or three . . ."

"We can settle that part later. The J.P. charge you anything?"

"Yes, he took twenty for the death certificates. We paid the air freight for the bodies already. Can we see them?"

"Yes, sure. Oh, I'm sorry, ma'am, forgot about the cold. Come on in. Here, let me get the light for you. There, okay now, right through here."

"Theo, I don't want to see them."

"What'd she say?"

"Says she doesn't want to see the bodies."

"Yeah. I can understand that, all right."

"Theo . . . I'll . . . I'll just hang back here, okay?"

"She staying there?"

"That's right."

"There's a chair if she wants it . . . Here, follow me. Now, how you going to get the bodies over to Colorado Springs from here?"

"In the pickup . . ."

"Can't do that."

"Oh?"

"State law, see."

"Yes, well . . . how much is it to take 'em over there?"

"It's more 'n eleven, I'll clue you."

"Yes . . . Well, can I pay you later? By money order?"

"Yeah? Well, I guess so. Sure. Here, here's my name and address."

"Thank you. You'll get your money. Want to shake hands?"

"Shake? Yeah, sure."

A soft nudge. "I'm sorry, Claudia, but it's time to go now. How do you feel?"

Smile. "Cold. You?"

Chuckle. "Yeah, me too. You're good folks, Claudia."

Smile. "What time will *they* get to Texas?"

"Tomorrow afternoon sometime . . . Angel's going to pick them up at the airport." Pause. And then, "Well, I guess we'd better get started. Check the door lock."

"Ah, you never did tell me about the pharmacist. Was he, was he *okay?*"

"Sure. It's all fixed up, and I still got the eleven on me."

"I wonder how the kids are? You know, I've been so worried about *this* that I just thought about the kids now, for the first time."

"Sure, me too . . . Don't feel bad, okay? We had enough to do just getting out here in the first place. The kids are fine, really. Let me have that map there."

"Want to sign right here?"

"Sure . . ."

"Thanks; say, those relatives of yours, by any chance?"

"No, they're some people killed in a wreck a couple of days ago."

"Oh, they're from out-a state, then?"

"Migrants."

"*Mi*grants?"

"Yeah, Mexicans from Texas up here for the harvest."

"I see . . ."

"Yeah."

"Well'p, see you."

"Right, sure . . ."

"Well, if we don't stop for anything but gas, I think we can make it by this evening. A straight shot. We won't get there *that* early, but we can make it . . . . You think we can buy some Velveeta for the trip?"

"No. I'd like to, but . . . what if we come up short on the trip?"

"Yeah; I guess so . . ."

"In the name of the Father and the S . . ."

"Yeah, the Father . . . Not much help on this trip, was He?"

"Theo . . . ah, where in *Missouri*, they say?"

"A place called Sedalia, Route 65 . . ."

"And they'll wait for us?"

"Sure . . . they got the kids."

"I'm worried . . ."

"They're okay, *really*. All set?"

"I guess so . . ."

"Well, Claudia, take a long, last look at Cheyenne Wells, Colorado."

"In the name of the Father . . ."

"Hey, John, you get your Mexicans off okay?"

"Yeah. I imagine they're on their way by now."

"Man, that was some wreck."

"Aha."

"And the in-laws? They left yesterday?"

"Guess so. Old man Fikes got twenty out of them for the death certificates. The man had eleven bucks on him when he came by my place. Woke up the wife and me."

"Yeah, I know. We sent 'em over. You charge 'em much?"

"Well, you can't squeeze blood as they say, but the way he grabbed my hand he probably could."

"Ha-'bout that? That's a good one, John."

"Yeah . . . see you, Dave."

"Yeah, right."

Señor and señora Esteban and Dorotea Múzquiz, natives of Bascom, Texas (Belken County) were killed in a one-vehicle accident (as the Pueblo *Chieftain-Star* put it) on the outskirts of Cheyenne Wells, Colorado; the migrant couple was on its way to the northern part of the state. Their pickup struck an embankment on the poorly-marked Route 365, and the Múzquiz couple were killed on impact.

The younger couple which came to claim the bodies, Teodoro Rivas and his wife, Claudia, were on the migrant trail to Mankato, Minnesota. After the identification, the town pharmacist-coroner-undertaker notified the Texas dependents by phone; these then called the migrant labor camp in Tulsa, Oklahoma where the Rivas couple had stopped overnight.

From there, then, the Rivas couple borrowed some money from their fellow Texans and headed for Cheyenne Wells; they were to meet in Sedalia, Missouri, two days later.

The Searchers V

Tom Purdy must be around sixty-years-old by now, in 1984; some twenty years ago, this high school English teacher from Pinconning, Michigan took a personal decision; small, by worldly standards, but solid and from the heart.

Unfortunately, and sad to say, I didn't know him as well as I would have wanted to; I met him and his wife by chance; a fluke. I do remember them well, though: quiet, strong, resolute.

Physically nondescript, I remember he had one of those so-called five o'clock shadows one used to read about years ago. And, Purdy would've had a magnificent mustache except for the School Board's ban against such things.

Mrs. Purdy was a schoolteacher as well; she was a little thing, but full of determination, as I discovered later on. Aside from teaching, she also gave her time to those clubs that are forever doing this and that.

The Purdys could just as easily have been Methodists as Presbyterians; the writer, by the way, has no basis for this assumption. They may have been Catholics for all the writer knows. But, it isn't important.

To the point. This simple, unassuming man, with very little money, too, decided on his own that something had to be done in re the squalid, barbaric, primitive housing provided (what a word!) for Texas Mexican migrant workers in southern Michigan. He sought no federal or state aid; on his own, then. Purdy spoke to his wife and so, both of them together with their two teenage sons, began to work on their own for a good number of people they'd never met and whose language they didn't speak. What it also cost them was time: time to talk with the growers (who turned out to be the owners as well) and it cost them some money (the Purdys' own) for them to buy roof shingles, concrete, electrical wiring, lumber, corrugated tin, paint, etc.

Tom Purdy's wife worked just as hard and as long as did the couple's teenage sons who gave up their own summer jobs; it took the Purdys the better part of two summers, and what they came up with wasn't palatial, to be sure, but then that hadn't been the idea, either. What they *did* do was to present the Texas Mexicans the opportunity to enjoy a measure of dignity much like that enjoyed in Texas: a clean, well-lighted place.

The Purdys accomplished what they set out to do but it took some doing: At first, of course, (of course) the growers called them Socialists, Reds, and the local press wrote a brief, ill-informed article which managed to ridicule their efforts and to belittle (that Jeffersonian word) that which the Purdys were trying to do.

Luckily for the Purdy family, and happily for the migrants, neither the federal nor the state governments had a hand in the project. The writer can well imagine what the outcome of *that* would have been . . . .

And that's about it. Tom Purdy, his wife (I doubt I ever learned her name), and their two boys did what they could, and they did it because they *wanted* to. That last part is hard to understand for some people, especially for those of us who suspect the worst of everybody.

The Purdys have no idea how much the writer appreciates them and what they did. To top it, the writer—who keeps poor notes—can't recall those Belken County people who worked the fields in '62–'63 when Tom Purdy decided to help his fellow men because they were that: his fellow men.

A Few Words

This section needed to be included here; the reason? It fits; that is, the writer—this writer—found it to be the proper place in this Chronicle of Klail City and its denizens. Not a case of premeditation, then. In writing, there's no telling what'll come up next unless one uses 3 x 5 cards; this writer can't use cards systematically. One of those things.

To add to this, the writer has no idea how many lives Rafe Buenrostro has gone through, and, because of that bit of ignorance, here he is again, much like he appears in *The Valley*.

* * * * * *

It was quite a surprise. Here we were, going from the 100% Texas Mexican North Ward Elementary to Klail's Memorial Jr. High and then, just like that, we ran across *other* mexicanos; we later found out that these had gone to South Ward, and they were different from us, somehow. Jehú Malacara, a cousin of mine, called them "The Dispossessed." Now, these mexicanos were one hell of a lot more fluent in English than we were, but they came up short on other things; on the uptake, for one, out on the playground, for another.

Example. When it came to handing out athletic equipment, we pushed and shoved as well as anyone; the American way, right? But these mexicanos hung back.

If our Texas Anglo classmates got the good footballs, we'd demand our share; not more. Equal; the American way. Naturally enough, the equipment manager—a bit of a pimp—tried to put the *chingas* to us, but a word to the wise is usually enough, and we told him way ahead of time that if a word wasn't sufficient, then push'd come to shove. Simple as that.

The first week, the assistant coach (no fool) would take note of the scrappiest kids and he'd tap us as prospects: "Say,

70

boy, how'd you like to play seventh grade football for Memorial?"

Some of us'd say yes and some would turn him down, but what we all noticed was that the docile mexicanos from South Ward usually hung back. Shy, kind-a.

* * * * * *

The shit who handed out the balls and gloves in physical education was called Betty Grable, by us, and to his face. Blond and a bit short in the leg, and a Mexican hater; plain as Salisbury. At first it seemed as if he'd save the worst equipment for us, but after a couple of weeks we were sure of it.

A word to the wise had not been sufficient. Three of us decided he needed convincing that we weren't ready or willing or able to take shit from him or anyone else. The American way.

But of course one *always* needs proof that one is being given the shortest end of the stick. Charlie Villalón was the first in line for a week, and he saw to it, but he still got the crap of the lot. When Charlie brought this to Betty Grable's attention at the beginning of the second week, all Charlie got was a pair of raised eyebrows and a sniff.

Well! Charlie, without a word, gave him a harsh lesson in civility; it would've cost Charlie two weeks expulsion, but the Coach fixed it, of course, and from then on, it was first come, first served. The American Way.

* * * * * *

One of the mexicanita transfers from South Ward, Conce Guerrero, was a Relámpago girl, a country girl.

Once, out of the blue, she said she'd known Jehú's parents. That Jehú's dad had died owing money at her grandfather's country store. It couldn't have been much, I don't imagine, but I *could* imagine what her merchant father must've said around the house on that account.

Jehú, had he got word of this, would've died from shame. Friends are friends where I come from, and so the secret stayed with me and with her, too.

Now, how was I to know I'd marry her a year after high school?

*   *   *   *   *   *

In our Junior year, Charlie Villalón was awarded a letter and a football jacket to go with it: K C in purple inside a white map of Texas. Young Murillo and I were given letters but no jackets. We were told we hadn't played enough quarters as per University Interscholastic League requirements. It was bullshit. The Texas Anglo kids *all* got sweaters or jackets. Oh, yes.

Well, came the following year and Coach Elmer "Nig" Hoskins came to class several times during spring training: "What's the matter, boys? How come y-all ain't out there running wind sprints and getting your licks like the rest of 'em?"

We told him.

Oh.

As dull as he was, he got the point; and, the school-board, somehow, came up with enough money for sweaters for all the eligibles.

It didn't mean much, really. In fact, it didn't mean a thing: Charlie Villalón and a couple of the other guys on the team died in Korea in 1951 at the Chongchon River crossing.

*   *   *   *   *   *

At Klail High almost everyone took shop or Ag; some of us took both. The shop guy wasn't a bad sort, but you couldn't

72

count on him; he'd take the easy way out if he could. As said, not bad, just weak.

During one of the field trips, one of the Texas Anglo guys made out like he had a fit or something, right in the bus. And then somebody else hid the bus keys.

Now, all of us had some sort of job or other after school and that meant we'd be late or lose the job, even. But that was okay; it was part of the fun of going to school. The keys turned up and the guy with the fit came to and old Simpkins, the shop guy, said not to worry: "We've got plenty of time, boys." Turned out he was wrong: damned bus came up flat 3 mi. out of Klail, and we had to run like hell to get to the jobs on time.

*   *   *   *   *   *

Territorial turf meant nothing at North Ward since most of us came from the same neighborhoods. It was different at Memorial Junior High and at the High, too. We noticed that the North Warders who'd made it to high school always sat on the gym steps; our legacy, then.

The South Ward mexicanos had no place to go; in limbo, as it were. To add to this, we made it a point to speak Spanish on the school grounds, even if it meant licks from the principal and detention hall, to boot.

*   *   *   *   *   *

When the World War II vets came home, many of us wanted to enlist right then and there. We were too young, of course, but we found we didn't have long to wait: Korea was just around the corner and later, among the dead, we counted David Leal, Ritchie Garza, Pepe Vielma, and Charlie Villa-lón; four from our graduating class alone.

*　*　*　*　*　*

In the Spring of Fifty-one, Cayo Díaz and I drove up to the cemetery in Seoul to read off the names on the temporary markers. I remember it well because Cayo and I took and drank up a case of Blue Ribbon Beer between us. And now, of course, every time I look at a can of Blue Ribbon . . .

*　*　*　*　*　*

Frozen Chosen. Once, three of us, Cayo Díaz again, and an underage kid named Balderas and I took part in a three-day shit job: fishing for the dead. The *fallen*, as the chaplain insisted on calling the dead.

Artillery fights could last two-three days without a let up. Many of the dead would wind up on the southbound rivers; ours and theirs, mixed and lumped together, bumping into each other . . . We'd wade in, waist high with G.I. poles and we'd stick 'em in the mud and hook the bodies floating by as they bobbed knocking heads together:

"Hey! It's one of theirs!"

Let it go.

"Hey, Sarge, over here . . . this one's ours . . . ."

Okay, just hold 'im there till I cut the dogtag. There, let 'im go . . . .

It was hell at first, but by late afternoon of the first day, people'd bet to see which unit collected more dog tags, winner take all.

At times, out of the blue, the names come back automatically: Poulter, Harkness, Gómez, Blair, Reese, Olivares . . .

*　*　*　*　*　*

Dead is dead, and that's what Charlie Villalón got in Korea; I remember the time Charlie got twenty licks from Coach

Schoenneman for copping a practice jersey. Taught Charlie a lesson, all right.

* * * * * *

As I recall, one, and only one, of the neighborhood guys became a priest; Gualberto Ornelas. A fat little guy and a helluva singer, too. His dad, after he lost a leg in a train accident, turned to making homemade candy for a living.

When some priests drove up one afternoon—black car, black soutanes (crows, my Aunt Mattie called them)—Mrs. Ornelas cried as Gualberto shook hands all around. Jehú and I looked at each other; my cousin shrugged and spit.

From then on, Sr. and Sra. Ornelas did as best they could, and I'd see them from time to time selling candy out at the race track, at the ball park, in front of the church . . . .

Years later—army, school, and work—I ran into Oblate of Mary Immaculate Gualberto Ornelas. I invited him to join old Father Pedro Zamudio and me for a beer at Dirty's. No, he couldn't, he said. Father Zamudio, shaking his head, predicted that Gualberto would never get to know his parish at all . . . .

A matter of time, I said.

Don Pedro: "No, Rafe; it's a matter of style. That boy'll never settle down."

* * * * * *

When the American school let out (I was in the third or fourth grade at that time), and provided one's folks stayed in the Valley for cotton picking, it was back to school in June and July; the neighborhood school run by Mexican national exiles. There, señor Bazán would lead us into the Mexican National Anthem:

Mexicans, at the cry of war . . .

This, of course, after nine months of *Texas, Our Texas* . . . . And here it was, June and July again: The *twos* tables, Rafe:

> dos por dos son cuatro
> dos por tres son seis . . .

And then: Jehú! ¿La capital de Albania?
Señor Profesor, la capital de Albania es Tirana . . .
And then, Mexico is an inverted horn of plenty! Look at the map!
From here we go to more class recitation:

> Man is an individual
> **MAN IS AN INDIVIDUAL!**

Gender?	Homo
Family?	Hominidae!
Species?	Mammalia!

> Man is distinguished from other animals
> specially because of his extraordinary
> mental development!
> Repeat it, please!

> . . . because of his extraordinary mental de-
> velopment!

Says who?
What-was-that?
¡Que sí, señor!
Ah . . . on your feet!

MEXICANS, AT THE CRY OF WAR . . .

Señor Bazán: (Rather sadly) ¡Hasta mañana, muchachos!

*   *   *   *   *   *

Swimming in the Rio Grande. It's ox-bow lakes, *resacas*; or out in the canals . . .

Last one in is horseshit!

And off we'd go out of the starting blocks. My brother Israel was the top swimmer, and it was he who pulled out Pepe Vielma when Pepe came up with a cramp. We ranged from twelve to sixteen, and no one said a word about Pepe's cramp when he walked back home that day.

Since Klail is surrounded by natural water canals, we'd go swimming there, too. At the Canal Grande, Young Murillo dove near one of the locks and he was the first to see the drowned boy rocking back and forth in the tall tules, a Klail City kid who'd run away early that summer.

At another time, near the waterfall, by the dam, we saw a grown-up who'd been more than half-eaten by the Río Grande garfish.

We couldn't have been very bright: we couldn't understand why we'd get whipped for going swimming without permission.

*   *   *   *   *   *

It's great being a kid. There's work, sure, but there's so much to see and do, too. Weddings, for instance; Texas Mexican weddings, what else?

Music, noise, people, Mexican and American beer, dancing, girls . . .

The year before my father died—was murdered, as I was taught to say—he took us all to the Vilches Ranch; my dad had led the commission asking for the girl's hand. She was to marry a relative of ours: Obdulio Yáñez, the He-Mare. Obdulio was a lump, my father said.

I was going on fourteen that summer, and I saw Conce Guerrero at the wedding. Nothing happened between us on a long walk we took, but it *looked* bad, and she got a reaming out. The following week, I walked from our ranch—El Carmen Ranch—to Relámpago, six miles away, and asked formally if I could see Conce and her mother. I explained that time got away from us, and that that was it.

A week later, at supper, my dad told me of Señora Margarita Guerrero's visit to *our* house: "Don Jesús, Rafe called on us last week. He was alone, and it was his idea to come calling." My Dad laughed and said she called me *un hombrecito serio*.

After supper, on the porch, I offered no explanation for my visit to the Guerrero family, and my Dad, who asked no questions, smiled first and then looked at me very seriously:

"Dame esa mano." Let's shake on it.

END OF ANOTHER LIFE OF RAFE BUENROSTRO

Brother Imás

Witnesses, witnesses, witnesses. All six or seven thousand of them had seen the late Bruno Cano go under rich Valley loam (and in sacred ground, to boot) and it must have been riding close to nine o'clock (CDT) when Father Pedro Zamudio and I finally headed for the parish house. It'd been a long funeral, but more on that later.

Father Pedro looked depressed, saddened, beat down, even; but appearances are merely that, and nothing more. The man of the cloth was aboil, and the targets of his wrath were at hand: Belken County (Texas Mexican sector), generally, and, specifically, the Carmona Brothers, Lisandro and Sabás. It was they—and no one else—who had led Don Pedro—and that's *led* not *lied*—and then convinced him to bury Bruno Cano in sacred ground after Cano and don Pedro had had a fatal but entertaining run-in the night before.

That night had started off with Bruno Cano and Melitón Burnias (that's Hard-luck Melitón) trying their hand and luck at coming up with some gold bullion said to be buried in doña Panchita Zuárez's backyard, or near there. For the record again: Doña Panchita is a curandera, a *healer*. She also earns part of "my living," as she calls it, mending broken hearts and virgos.

Cano and Burnias were unsuccessful (as so many others before them), but it wasn't the failure that caused Bruno Cano's myocardial infarct; the man was a business man and used to failure. No. The infarct was due to a helluva fright and to an even worse temper fit directed at don Pedro Zamudio who had refused (God's truth) to help Cano out of the ad hoc hole which he (Cano) and Burnias had dug.

Don Pedro and Cano came to hard words, and when Cano insulted don Pedro's mother, the priest refused to bury his old friend. No, no, and not on sacred, either.

The Carmona brothers prevailed, however, and took charge of the funeral. To the point: less of a funeral, more of an entertainment—a foofaraw—and the damn thing took seven hours. Four choirs and everything . . . .

And here we were, don Pedro and I, seven hours later, heading for the parish house. Evening had come but the sun was visible still at nine o'clock, and it was hot; July-August hot. The first thing that came off was the collar.

"Here," he said. Then the soutane and again, "Here, Jehú." And then his jacket and, since I was already carrying the ornamental funeral candles and candleholders and that big old Bible, well!, I couldn't keep up as he quickened his pace and that temper of his, too. The breathing was a fright, and the fury was now zeroed in on the one target of opportunity: the Carmona brothers . . . .

Don Pedro was working on one of those sermons of his, and here I was, sweating, lagging behind, being yelled at, out of breath, hungry, and thinking of having to hear that fire and brimstone that night at supper and then for six regular masses plus the evening mass at a ranch mission as well.

As acolyte, I was as much a prisoner as the Flora parishioners. And would they show on Sunday? Of course! Would the Carmonas show? Sure, it was don Pedro's turn to get even and while Flora people are many things (and one can convict 'em of being dull most of the time) but they're not rude. They'd show, and they'd take their punishment, too. No need to say that they'd wait for another chance to get at the mission priest who, after all, was Flora-born and raised. (Oh, if Rome knew what went on in the outside world away from the view and sight of *L'Osservatore* . . .)

The thought of Old Chana's supper kept me afloat, but barely. To add to this, I'd have to bolt the food if I wanted to sneak out that night. The sneaking out would be easier this time since don Pedro's mind was on vengeance (Romans xii, 19) and I wouldn't have to worry about Chana's tattling this time.

We walked in and Chana spoke first: "Supper's on the table, and the limeade is as cold as it's going to get."

I'd spotted her at the burial site, and she knew I had. I winked at the old fraud, but she pretended otherwise and turned the glasses upward and filled them. She busied about doing nothing, avoiding my stare at any cost, and then went out to the front porch.

Don Pedro ate in silence, but I noticed he ate well enough. I was on my firsts when he rose (without a word of thanks for the meal) and went to his room, slamming the door behind him. I waited for a few seconds, and then I heard his voice, a low rumble at first and then that clear baritone, and finally the words started coming out here and there, and choice ones, too. The parishioners were among the first casualties, then the town of Flora came under fire, after that the Valley went up in flames. At every inch of the way, though, the Carmona brothers and Bruno Cano were put to death, sent to Hell, resurrected, and put to death again. Don Pedro was working on the sermon and enjoying it for once. "Seven hours! Seven! You sinners! No lunch, no *merienda*, and no supper either. No bathrooms! Prisoners all!"

I wanted to hear more, but I also wanted to go downtown, and I did. After all, I'd hear the sermon from first mass on, and by then the sermon would be polished to a high gloss and served to the cream of Flora society which, in turn, would sit there and take it and love very minute of it. They're incorrigible.

But, by the time that Sunday rolled around, I was no longer living in Flora; between the time of the funeral and Sunday, a matter of four days, I was off and running again, this time with Brother Imás: A Preacher whose Persuasion was Protestant (sicut) and whose itinerary was variable and whose calling constant (sicut, bis).

The Brother was named Tomás and thus answered to Tomás Imás. (Some parents have gone nose first and straight to Hell for less). According to him, he had abandoned His Humble Hearth to follow the Lord's Path, Preaching Precious Parables to Philistenes and other livestock that had wandered, raced, or strayed from the Lord's Lovely Light. (We may as well stop right here; it could be because of his name or because of personal, peculiar, or particular preferences—and I believe it's catching—but Brother Imás was a card-carrying alliterationist).

Brother Imás was keenly interested, first of all, in saving people from the Fiery Pits and, secondly, and on a dietary note, on eating at least one hot meal every day. Since he worked in the Valley and specialized in the mexicano branch of Christianity, the pickings were far from lean: the Valley mexicanos had already been stretched in the matters of credulity and belief and faith first in 1836, then in 1848, and subsequently, as well. As for feeding one's fellow, well!, this is plain good manners and customs, isn't it? The Valley mexicanos solved Life's Great Problem years ago: Deny neither food nor comfort to anyone, and when it comes to salvation, women and children first. After that, it's every man for himself.

It just so happens (so to speak) that on that Thursday after the funeral, I was on my way to doña Panchita Zuárez's lot, shovel in hand, and ordered to cover up the hole dug up by Bruno Cano and Hard-luck Melitón. As you've read, this was the hole where Cano's heart collapsed on him. It was one of those days where it looks like rain and then it *doesn't*, and that may explain why the heat wouldn't let up for a minute. Since I had the entire day to carry out the chore, I'd stop here and there, greeting a friend here and a friend there when I spotted Edelmiro Pompa talking with a man; an outsider, a *fuereño*, as we say in the Valley. And there he was: black-suited, a white, buttoned-down shirt, no tie, wearing one-a those hard, flat, wide-brimmed straw hats popular back in the Thirties, and talking to Edelmiro.

When I walked up to them, they were talking in Spanish and then I heard the *fuereño* say: O, bless-ed, when you growing up, you will be seeing how important are education and the benefits, or something like that. The words were in Spanish, all right, but that intonation! And the pronunciation! He *looked* Mexican, as Anglos say, but as soon as he opened his mouth and that Spanish came out . . . well, whatever it was, it was unique to a degree.

I looked at him a while longer, and I noticed that he stood with his hands behind his back which was okay, too, but he didn't rock back and forth like a grown up, and he didn't use his hands much either. He then crossed his arms and even *that* didn't look right. An outsider, then, no two ways about that. Edelmiro hadn't said a word for a while; he kept his eyes on the *fuereño* making up his mind about something, it looked like.

Edelmiro'd shake his head just a bit and didn't even return my "howdy" when I came up to them. I finally got between them and Edelmiro pointed with his lips and said: "What do you think?"

The *fuereño* threw out his hand and I caught it as he said: "One of God's Good Guests, Tomás Imás. I Sing and Say Psalms for Salvation."

"Lo . . . (I got my hand back), Jehu Malacara; I just live here is all."

"And that shovel? You're a worker?"

"Oh . . . I'm on my way to cover up a hole; a big hole."

"A big hole? For a dead Christian?"

"Afraid so, yes. The thing is that the dead person isn't in the hole, though."

"There must be a logical explanation, youngster. A basis of historical reasoning for covering an empty hole?"

"It's a fairly long story, sir; I'm not sure I know where to begin . . . . You weren't here yesterday, by any chance?"

"Oh, yes, I, your newest friend, was present. But I was

83

alone in this deserted town. Present and all alone and alone until night fell when I see the townsmen late at night."

"The town was deserted because everyone from Flora was at the funeral. Isn't that right, Edelmiro?"

"Right. Jehu and I here are acolytes, and we were at the funeral."

"Funeral . . . and who is dying and getting buried, youngsters?"

"A man named Bruno Cano."

"He owns the Golden Fleece, the slaughterhouse."

"And his bereaved wife? Her whereabouts?"

"Aw, she's dead; been dead, right, Jehu?"

"Ah-hah."

"Oh? And where do you do your work?"

"I work for don Pedro Zamudio."

Edelmiro: "That's the priest I told you about."

"The village priest?"

"Well, sort-a; the mission priest."

"Well now, I too toil the vineyards of the Creator."

"You mean you're a priest?" Edelmiro.

"Lutheran priest, a Preacher of Precious Parables."

"Are you a holy-roller?"

(Softly) "Geez, Edelmiro; that's a dumb . . ."

"Why? What's wrong with it?"

"I'm a priest. A Preacher of the Perpetual Pronouncements of Providence."

"He's a roller, all right."

"And you are being an acolyte, you say?"

(Softly) "How do you like his Spanish, Jehu?"

"Yes. I . . . I . . . I help out in the mission . . . but I also run errands, sweep out stores, and once I worked in a carny troupe."

"You are having no parents, then?"

"That's right; I'm an orphan, but I'm Valley-born, and I've got friends and relatives here."

"Youngster, I am spending this Friday here, and tomorrow I am on my way to Klail City. You want to be my assistant? Want you, then, to Search for the Salvation of Souls and the Sweeping of Sins under the Soil? No, answer not as yet, you continue with your shovel work, and tomorrow you decide, for tomorrow is Friday, the Fairest Day of the Faithful."

"Well, I . . . who's to know what will happen tomorrow?"

"Only God, that's true."

(In the meantime, Edelmiro breaks in: You want a ride to doña Panchita's? We can ride double.)

"Okay . . . ah, Brother?"

"Please?"

"I gotta go now, ah, I'll see you."

"No doubt."

"What'd he say his name was? *Más* y *más*, more and more?"

"I dunno, Miro, that's what it sounded like to me too."

"Lemme tell you this, old don Pedro better not hear you been chinning with no holy roller 'cause . . ."

"Ha! Two weeks ago, a week ago, yeah. Now? Forget it. Right now he's thinking about getting back at the Flora types come Sunday."

"On account of the funeral? Really?"

"Well, what did you expect?"

"Well . . . ha! that was quite a crowd out there, wadn't it?"

"I'll say . . . and I'll say this now: you-all from Flora don't miss a lick; and I'll tell you this, too: wait'll Sunday! Yessir. Come Sunday and don Pedro's gonna . . . ah, which mass you want to work?"

"Oh, I don't care . . . . What'cha got?"

"Well, I'm working the six, seven, and the eight o'clocks . . . . I'll eat at nine and serve on the ten o'clock and the eleven High Mass."

"Look! Over there . . . there's doña Panchita . . . Let's see what she's up to . . . Ah, before I forget, put me down for the eight and nine and I'll work with you on the High."

"Good . . . we're gonna need two more for the High, now. Nice morning, miz Panchita."

"Isn't it, though? And what brings you out to this neck-a the woods?"

"That hole, and here's my shovel."

"And I see you've got yourself an assistant, too."

"Naw, he just gave me a ride is all."

"Well, if you want me to, I can help."

"And where're you off to, Miz Panchita?"

"To the herb store, kids. I need some balm gentle and some other stuff. I'll be back, and I'll leave you here with God."

"Yes, and a good-bye to you, Miz Panchita."

"Bye, Miz Panchita."

"Really, Jehu, I'll help, and then we can go to the River; whadda-ya say to that?"

"No, I better not, I really got to get to this, you know."

"I'll help; I'll spell you, really."

"Man! It's getting hot, you know."

"Okay, Miro; say no more. You're bushed, right?"

"Yeah; it's heavy going here."

"Well, we're about half done, I think."

"Come on, Jehu; let's leave it for now. Come on . . . let's hit that River."

"Okay, but we gotta come back to this."

"Sure, sure."

Sure, sure. Well, I didn't finish the job. What with going swimming with Edelmiro, stumbling across Señor Mata's watermelon patch and sneaking a smoke, time just flew right on by. It's that Daylight Saving Time; the sun finally went down, and when it did, so did Anacleta Villalobos, except she went down in the hole, and—wouldn't you just know it?—she broke her damn leg. Anacleta is like that; she's an only child (and that's just an expression); she's also the pride and joy, the apple of, and etc. of her father don Jacobo, aka, *Scorpio*.

His child is nearing forty; she's a bit on the arid side, too, and minus a steady boy-friend; another expression. She didn't even live close to that neighborhood, but there she was, looking for Miz Panchita in the never-say-die hope of locating some good news via the tea leaves; a man, some hope of one, or perhaps going o-for-four again. Cleta must've been looking at the future because what she didn't see was the hole. She plain missed it—and that *is* an expression—when down she went and there she stayed. For the count; that was some fall that was.

I received the news faster'n than fast: Edelmiro and I were finally on our way back from the Río Grande and we were tugging with the shovel when a grown-up said: "Don Pedro's hunting for you. Crazy Cleta got a broke leg; fell into Bruno

Cano's hole, and . . ."

I remember extending my right arm and handing Edelmiro the shovel, and the next thing I knew I was running down to the Klail City-Flora Bridge. I must've run all the way and as hungry as I was, I still fell asleep almost immediately.

God came through again: another glorious Valley sunrise, the Gulf mist rising just high enough to form a rainbow that lasted an hour or more. When the sun drove the mist and the clouds away, I decided to cross the highway to sit under a chinaberry tree. If Brother Imás was really going to Klail City, he'd have to pass through here; there wasn't any other way . . . .

Around midday (and I'd missed three meals by then) I spotted him, and I waited for him under the chinaberry tree; when he drew up, I told him I was ready, and he didn't say a word. Instead, he looked at me for a while, reached for his knapsack, and produced two navel oranges from it. Again, without a word, he handed me the larger orange and we started out that clear, cloudless July day leaving Flora and a trail of orange peels on our way to Klail City.

"Jehu?"

"Yes, brother."

"In the Name of the Lord."

"Amen."

A Newborn Sun

The Texas Mexican waltz *Messenger Dove, Fly and Tell (The One I Love and Wait For)* written by master songwriter Epaminondas Olivares shares the same tune with two of Brother Imás's favorite hymns: *Innocent Shepherd, Guard Thy Flock,* and *Place This Hand in Thy Sacred Wound.* These, the hymns, are found on pp. 37 & 43, resp., of the hymnal *His Holy Hymns* pub. by Biechner Publishers of Oshkosh, Wisc. Brother Imás had sixteen copies of the hymnal as well as three other books and all of which were secured by a no. 4 fishing line cord. The other books were *The New Testament* with a Spanish trans. provided by ABC Translators also of Oshkosh; Suetonious's *Twelve Caesars,* in paperback; and *Poco a Poco,* the second book fo Spanish grammar used in some Valley private (Mexican) schools. All of this, and more, fit in one of the knapsacks which he carried with him.

The day I joined him, he removed an empty knapsack from a sidepocket of the full one, and thus we loaded mine up with books and some navel oranges as well as cheese parings, rennet, junket, and *pan blanco* given him by the Flora faithful.

We ate two of the navels in silence and continued our march to Klail. At that time, Brother Imás must've been around thirty years old, and his face and hands wore that perpetual brown toast of the outdoorsman. The straw hat I spoke of earlier was either on his head or in hand when he used it as a fan, but wherever it was, it was never out of sight. Months later, in the winter time, I discovered he owned and used one of those old-timey aviator caps; the ones with the side flaps that Capt. Rickenbacker and Frank Luke sported in The Great War. He owned but two pair of trousers, both black, and three white-on-white shirts; two of these were short-sleeved and one was a half-sleeved. Truth to tell, all three had been long-sleeved shirts when new. His suit jacket was a light-weight one and it too was dark and made of cotton. He wore the one pair of shoes and these, ankle high, had double soles, storm welts, what we call *viboreros*, snake protectors, and were pretty well worn but not down or out.

My own wardrobe was as fine as his although there wasn't as much of it: shoes, one pair and worn only when absolutely n., a pair of khaki trousers and another one made of jeancloth and cut much like the khakis. Two of my shirts were the short-sleeved, pull-over type and the third one was a gift from don Pedro Zamudio himself: white, long-sleeved which was meant, exclusively, for wakes and weddings. And, we both went without socks as a matter of course and convention.

It was quite the forced march from Flora to Klail City, and we arrived there at nightfall. It was also a long and hard march, but worth it: we had sized each other up and got to know one another well. I held back some, though, but now, years later, I find that he learned more than I suspected at the time. For his part, however, he told me his life story up to the time we had met on the previous day. I learned even more, but I didn't realize this until years later when destiny or whatever got us together again briefly. (This part I speak of was prior to his losing his left leg below the knee through necrosis as a result of a fanging by a common Valley rattler.)

Brother Imás was an Albion, Michigan-born Mexican. His grandparents hailed from Parras, Coahuila, México, and emigrated to the United States as many others before and after them as a consequence of the Mexican Revolution. The family crossed the Río Grande (all of them: the entire family) and settled, lightly, in Texas, before moving on to Illinois first and then on to Michigan. The family worked up and down the Midwest for years until the grandparents opted for Chicago's *La garra* district where so many mexicanos have lived and worked and died. The children grew up, married, and left the Home's Humble Hearth (Brother I.) and began scattering and strewing kids all over the place. Brother Imás's father, e.g., married and moved back to Albion and from there to Saginaw and then south and west to Kalamazoo and Marshall (and wherever there was work to be found),and, finally, back to Albion where Tomás, an only son among seven daughters, delivered papers as a kid.

English was the language and the order of the day. He didn't speak Spanish as a child up in Michigan with his old man. Brother Imás claimed he understood it fairly well since he heard it both at home and from other mexicano families in Albion and out in Adrian, Michigan, as well. His father stopped working in the fields (cherry, cucumbers, grapes, and beets) and hooked on with a construction company as a laborer; by dint of hard work and some luck, too, he became an electrician's helper; this was the first indoor work he'd done in his life, and he liked it. From this, he went on to Auto-Lite and then with the Chevrolet Steering Gear works in Saginaw, and finally, he opened up his own electrical shop in Albion from where he started off some years before.

By this time, Brother Imás was going on sixteen and had never seen the inside of any church. At seventeen, he joined the Army right out of high school; he was sent to Fort Custer, there in Michigan, where he swore mightily to defend the country and its constitution. He took the oath in one of those two-story barracks that the Army—whenever it damn well pleases—converts into chapels, churches, temples, whatever.

He spent the next two years in the military between Forts Custer and Benjamin Harrison; the latter, at that time, in the northern part of Indianapolis, a city of homes and churches which also claimed some two-hundred whorehouses, according to those who know of such things. That last datum came as a bit of a shock to the writer, but it was there, in Indianapolis, that Brother Imás ran into two Mormons (ties, white shirts, bikes) who were doing their two-year hitch in service for the Church in Indianapolis.

With Honorable Discharge papers in hand, Brother Imás

made for Dearborn, Michigan, to sign up as an apprentice welder with the Ford Motor Co. On the religion side of things, he took to Mormonism for a while but soon after left the sect to hook up with some Pentecostals who were gathering strength through numbers in Dearborn at the same time. Then, one-two-three, just like that, he quit the job with Ford to become a pillar of the local Pentecostal church. And, not long after that, he hopped on a bus, arrived in Albion and announced to his parents that he was off, off to the Southern states, of all places, to sell Bibles to them who sorely needed them, he said. His travels took him to both Carolinas and Virginia and on through Kentucky, Tennessee, Georgia, Florida, etc.

Love showed up and came calling in the Peach State and Brother Imás flirted with the idea of marriage, but he left it at that. He claims that this made him a firmer adherent to the religious cause and so he took himself and his Bibles from Atlanta to Montgomery, Ala., where he ran into a Hazel-type who was also a full-time Bible salesman and who happened to be at the same bus station at the same time. Well, one thing led to another, and this is how Brother Imás learned of a school in Racine, Wisconsin, that specialized in evangelism, prosletyzing, and preaching.

He spent two weeks in Montg. and he then packed up the remaining Bibles on hand, drew out a money order and sent both books and money order to his employers up in Michigan. This done, he headed for Albion once again; the upshot of all this is that he spent a month with his parents and told them he was now ready to begin his life as a victim and lover of God, and that he was on his way to Racine, Wisc. His parents, Mexican-raised and thus adherents to laissez-faire, wished him well, pressed a few dollars on him, and so one must assume that love and respect were in long supply in that household.

So, he started his studies, *con ahinco* as we say, firmly and with purpose, but the curriculum (doing good, helping the fallen, loving one's neighbor as one's self, etc.) was something he already knew and had lived as well for the past two-three years there. He dropped out before the first year was out, but he was most grateful (and said so) for the time and patience given him. One of the things he did pick up was a working knowledge of Spanish learned from an Anglo-Swedish couple who'd done some long and hard time in the Valley.

The couple, after logging some twelve years in Belken County, returned to their Wisconsin Synod headquarters, and dedicated their efforts to train others to serve as preachers for a newly-founded lode of Lutherans among the Texas Mexicans in the Valley. The couple had more than merely earned their way to Heaven, but now it was up to another generation to do the same. Brother Imás learned that unique Spanish of his from the couple, and the very first thing he did was to go right back to Albion to try it out on his father. Well! Brother Imás reported that both parents were pleasantly and then quite surprised at his usage; I believe this, having been exposed to it myself.

When we finally sat down for our first chat that day we trouped out of Flora, we did it under some heavy huizache trees that gave both shade and protection against the Belken sun which is like no other in fierceness. As said, the last half of the conversation was done at a walk, but at a steady clip and not once did Brother I. raise a finger in his hand to ask for a ride; not once. Later on when we got to know each other well, he told me he hadn't hitched a ride on purpose: he was testing me, he said. He wanted to find out on his own and without me telling him if I had the right stuff, if I could walk without complaining. Since I hadn't quit on him, that created a bond that lasted until I settled in Klail, and he moved on out to Jonesville-on-the-Rio where, years later, he lost that left leg of his to that rattler.

That same first night, though, we found a place to stay; the back of Mr. Villalpando's garage, where he kept the tires used as trade-ins. We began to eat some of the parings and I remember we overate some. He had his eyes closed, his smallish hands on his smaller stomach and he began to hum a familiar tune, and I joined right in there.

Surprised, he stopped, looked at me and said:

"Why, Jehu, you do know the *Innocent Shepherd*."

"What's that?"

"The song, Jehu; the hymn that sounds like *Place o' Lord Your Holy Hand on Me*."

"Sorry, Brother, but there's some mistake somewhere; I mean, what you and I were humming there was an old-timey waltz called *The Carrier Pigeon*."

"Oh, no, Jehu . . . not at all."

"Oh, yes; Brother. I know that song as well as I know myself. My dad taught it to me. He used to play it on the accordion."

"Accordion? Your father was a philarmonic, then?"

"Is that anything like a farmer? 'Cause if it is, that's what he was, you know. He played the 'cordion for fun; learned it by himself, my father did."

"Self-taught, then?"

"Yeah, that's it. Couldn't smell, buy, or read a note, but he could play 'em. And fast, too."

"And . . . and you say that the song is a waltz about doves?"

"Doves, pigeons; there must be over twenty verses of eight lines each to it. I knew a bunch at one time."

"Strange . . ."

"It may be, but I knew 'em, and the tune's the same, all right."

"Well, Jehu, I learned the waltz at the evangelical school; I learned it from Mr. and Mrs. Edmundsen."

"The couple who taught you that Spanish of yours?"

"One and the same, yes."

"Well, I guess that's it, then . . . They lived down here for many years from what you say, and I bet they just took the music by Maestro Olivares."

"Took? Take? Ah, no, Jehu, they are honest people."

"Friends of yours are friends of mine, Brother Imás, so we'll change the *took* to *borrowed*. How's that? We'll say they borrowed the notes and then added new words."

"Sacred words, Jehu, that serve our fellow man."

"Amen."

"Good, Jehu, good, good . . . Since you know the melody, you and I can sing it together."

"You mean now? Right now? Here?"

"Well, yes; unless you think we'll disturb somebody."

"Oh, there's no danger a-that here with the tires and all."

"Well, here's the book; open it to page thirty-seven and then we'll do hymn forty-three. Ready?"

"Here we go."

Well, sir, we commenced a-singing, as they say, and I'd sing melody or he would and there we were until I got those hymns down pat, and I said I'd teach him the *Tantum Ergo* in Latin, and this took him to Martin Luther—a great man, he said—and then I said I'd teach him a hymn in Spanish sung in the Valley, the one about *I Raise My Voice on High to Laud Thee Only, Lord*, and which, by the way, was don Pedro Zamudio's favorite of favorites. Brother Imás never said die, and then I taught him others as time went on in Klail City.

Note: When the Brother and I spoke *solus*, he didn't rhyme or make use of alliterations. This was natural talk, and the other was the public voice; the public persona, as it were. Now, he never did explain (and I didn't ask, by the way) why it was he spoke one way and then the other, but I guess he did it for effect. A way of getting attention, see? That *sui generis* pronunciation, however, was as constant and as unique as the sun whose rays we etc.

Well, we sang the night away, and it was agreed we'd and there I go, rhyming again) both go see don Manuel, the one cop in Klail, about public preaching and singing so as to keep within the law. I did explain to the Brother that since I had worked in Klail City with the carny troupe, that there were some people who knew me. And vice versa. Since he didn't say word one to that, I went on to say that I was blessed— BLESSED—with a fine memory, and that if he wanted to teach me some prayers, why, I'd learn them and give the people a sermon or two. His ears raised a bit on that one and he said that tomorrow was another day (which it was) and that we'd both start working in the vineyards of the Lord.

"Jehu, in the name of the Lord, you may go to sleep."

"Amen, Brother."

"Amen."

With Brother Imás

"No one who has had his testicles crushed or his penis cut off shall marry into the Lord's community . . . . That, ladies and gentlemen from Belken County, is what Saint Deuteronomy says, yes!, and he said it right there in the Bible! *Our* Bible, the very one . . . Yea! Listen to this, dear brothers in and of the faith, hark! Hear what the saintly Saint Deuteronomy also tells us: You may eat any clean bird, but the following are the ones of which you must not eat: the griffon, the vulture, the eagle, the buzzard, and the kite in all its several species.

"Well? What-do-you-say-to-*that*? Now, the Bible isn't going to lie, is it? And, it presents us with advice . . . good, sound advice, yes! As sound as the one I've just quoted for you. Are you in doubt? Have you been cursed with bad luck? Do you seek the love of that special someone? Listen to this: Seek and you shall find all the answers in this sacred book . . .

"So you don't read English, is that what's holding you back? Ha!, I say. Think of your salvation friends: you need not understand what you read to be saved! Are you listening? Let me hear you say AMEN!"

AMEN!

"That's it . . . this old, I say and I repeat myself, this old, ancient even, this old testament has the power, yes! The power and the glory of the written word! Yes, yes, yes. Salvation and the road to salvation may be yours by having this book in your possession, at home, on the job, oh yes . . . What a miracle, people. Do you hear?"

YES.

"This tender tome, today, tomorrow, practices, preaches, and protects us here and hands us happiness for the entire hamily . . . ah, family!"

FAMILY!

"Look at this sample, see, in my right hand, the hand of the heart, the hand of truth: 'Oh, get thee behind me, Satan; all flesh is grass.' Yes!

"Look! Listen! Take this book home, you gentle people of Bascom . . . Now!

"To repeat, it doesn't matter if it's in English; not at all. What *does* matter is the *act*; the act, the grand gesture, *not* the translation that *P*erpetual *P*rovidence *P*rovides for us as we walk those-oh-so-long-and-narrow bridges to ETERNAL HELL, but why listen to *me*? Let me read what Job says to Eliphaz: 'No eye shall see me; And he puts a veil over his face. He digs through houses in the darkness.' Here, here, here allow me to translate:

"El ojo (eye) que mire (that sees) pondrá (will put) buena cara (a good face) a las casas (to the houses) que tengan este texto (of darkness).

"No, my dear brethren, no, the Bible doesn't lie. And how could it? And if I, a child of fifteen, am a messenger, it's because I've seen the light and I know the way . . . . I'm an orphan, yes!, but not orphaned of faith, no! The messenger! *Take* those well-written wondrous words, partake of faith, fellowship, and felicity. Now!"

NOW!

"Thank you. A quote! Yes, a final quote: 'Is this Naomi? Is this Naomi? Is this Naomi?' The answer to *that* is in the book of Samuel, and I—Jehú Malacara—a native of Relámpago, Texas, just down the road there, have found the answer. But! It wasn't easy, no. I worked and labored, long and hard, here and there, and everywhere. But I was lost! And then? Lost and found. Yes, a servant to the reverend Father Pedro Zamudio from Flora—a saintly man—and through him I saw the light, and I saw the way; I memorized the Bible, with special care for the Old Testament and respect for the New one . . . . The Old one is old, but more than old, it's a testament!

Amen. Secretum Secretorum. Poridat de Poridades. Amen. Amen."

AMEN!

That, then, was part of my life with the sainted Tomás Imás,

> Lutheran believer
> of sainted breast;
> Strong deliverer,
> though humbly dressed,

when I sold Bibles up and down and in Belken County.

He had sold Bibles years before in Tenn., Ala., Ga., the Carolinas, etc., but he'd done it door-to-door, and that's a killer. Now here, in Belken County, it's too hot for door-to-door selling, as I told him. You've got to get folks in a crowd, bunched up, see, like on Saturdays when they come in for groceries and such. So, after my spiel, I'd step down and hawk the stuff face-to-face.

It sure didn't take me long to see that I was going to waste my time talking to the men; it was the women who'd do the buying. A smile helps, of course. But, good quality helps too; solid buckram, good, clear paper, the ink black and uniform; nothing cheap, those Bibles. We charged them $3.00 per book and this proved to be a fair price as well as affordable.

The profit was enough to insure that we'd each eat at least one hot meal a day; who could want more?

We'd done well in Bascom, and Edgerton was next on this go-round. Brother Imás kept his hands down as we walked;

no hitchhiking again, but it wasn't meant to be Edgerton: he had spotted a roadside cottonfield and said he'd take the Word right to where the hands were going at it. And it was there that that common Valley rattler made a grab for his leg.

As mentioned earlier, he lost part of the leg below the knee, and after a fairly long convalescence (which the Wisconsin Lutheran Synod covered, by the way) he went to live and work in Jonesville-on-the-Rio. He kept up the preaching end of it, all right, but no more traveling, he decided. Jonesville's always enjoyed a good-sized crop of Mexican Protestants, and Brother Tomás Imás regarded the snake bite as a sign for him to stay put in Jonesville. It was a good sign, I said, but *I* hadn't gotten it since it was meant for him.

The following year, P. Galindo helped Brother Imás get a ride to Albion, Mich. Kara-mel Jara was going up, and he and P. and some truckers got together, selected the truck and the route for him. One of the truckers said he was going as far as New Buffalo, Michigan and that was enough: from there, all Brother Imás had to do was to hop on a bus to Albion where his folks'd be waiting for him . . . . He did so, grateful to the end, of course, and I lost sight of this fine man for some time.

For my part, I fell ill for a while there, but after I recovered—nothing serious—I headed for Klail and landed there like a cat: on my feet and working at my Uncle Andy's gaming hall. I worked there until I hooked on as a goatherd part of the summer at don Celso Villalón's ranch. (A word on don Celso: he sported two nicknames, The Tiger of Santa Julia and Buckshit, and not Buckshot as some people think. Why Buckshit? Because the man dearly loved to fire a shotgun he himself had sawed off years ago. No reason to fire, he said, just liked the sound of it. As he said to no one in partic., "I can afford it. So what the hell?"

A couple of months later, don Manuel Guzmán drove up to the Villalón ranch and drove me back to Klail.

"You're going to school, boy, and you're staying with my wife and me. I'll see about a job later on . . . ."

And I did, and I got to see Rafe Buenrostro and the other guys. What I didn't know was that don Víctor Peláez had remembered me in his will. It wasn't much, but the idea of being remembered was enough for me to settle down, to give it my level best at Klail High.

At My Uncle Andy's
General Sweep and Gambling Table Boy

As soon as Brother Imás decided to head out to Jonesville-on-the-Río after a five-month stint in Klail City, I opted to stay in Klail, and as I did so, my Uncle Andy took me in at his gambling hall, one of those open-air places of sin found in Baptist Texas. It happens.

Uncle Andy quoted Livy in re a man's personal habits being his own but this didn't set right with his wife, my Aunt Aureliana. He smoked a bit and drank less, but he had set his goal toward populating part of Klail and most of Bascom and Flora in his lifetime. The issue was a strange variety of jetsam and this, again, made my Aunt Aureliana difficult to live with. Considering.

About the time Rommel was driving Churchill and the Eighth Army to distraction and admiration, my relatives were in their fifties and love, as we say, was a word heard elsewhere.

As said, my uncle owned the place, but he didn't operate it actively; for this he'd hired two of his illegitimate sons, Felix Bustos, the day man, and Domingo Loera, the night shift. The den was a two-room affair placed at mid-alley off Hidalgo Street. You'd never catch him cross-armed and standing behind the bar or wetting wiping-rags to wipe the chalk marks off the domino tables. He was busy on other matters; skirting the issue or, as he said, *en asunto de faldas*.

Nothing to running the place since it was an all-drink, no-food situation, and it was here, years later, that the following took place:

It had become a beer joint then, different name, different owner and everyone with twenty years on all our backs and faces. Ernesto Tamez up and broke and smashed a 6 x 6 foot mirror during the course of a three-day drunk, tear, bat, or as we say: *una parranda de falda afuera y de bragueta abierta*. Polín Tapia had painted a blowsy nude, and then Ernesto Tamez came along and threw a half-full quart of Pearl Beer at it. Well now, Lucas Barrón—Dirty Luke—he jumped across the bar and sent Ernesto Tamez skidding across the glass and under a table; he stayed there, too. Wouldn't come out. Some ten to five minutes later, Ernesto's two older brothers showed up; Emilio the Gimp tried to tough it out, but Dirty Luke, he snatched and grabbed a heavy mop handle, broke it in half, and then whacked the Gimp bam! you shit! Take *that* and don't ever say I never give you nothin'. Emilio the Gimp's been deaf from that day on. Right after that, Joaquín, that's the oldest of the Tamez men, looked at the glass on the floor, threw a glance first at Emilio and then at Ernesto, and—without a word—picked up his brothers and took them home.

About a month later, another nude, and this, too, was Polín Tapia's handiwork; Joaquín Tamez had paid for *all* damages, spot cash, too, and then bought drinks for all the regulars at the *Aquí me quedo Bar*. The nude, through no coincidence, resembled that great and serious whore, La güera Fira.

My Uncle Andy's place was called The Oasis; the front room was a domino-playing section. The backroom was a more serious matter: baccarat, peep and turn, blackjack, thirty-one, etc. Not much talk going on in that one since gaming is serious play. I *liked* working there, and I went from table to table collecting a dime from the winner, and after every fifth game, I'd collect a nickel from each player. This, of course, was Uncle Andy's vigorish. He, in turn, supplied the cards, the dominoes, the chalk, and guaranteed the following: no women and no music. It was better than home, he said.

Don Manuel Guzmán, the cop, played a damn good hand at

baccarat, cooncan, and was considered an ace at American poker, *póker americano*, as *draw* is called there. Don Manuel's presence insured that no trouble or hell-raising would be tolerated: the man liked quiet games, with friends.

Don Manuel tolerated my presence there; he'd known my folks for years and he was always after me to finish school and such. This was summer now and I could rest from that quarter. He meant well, and he wanted to place me with the Torres family, a nice, good family, everyone said, and they were, too, but I wanted to be on my own that summer; again.

One morning, just like that, I packed up and decided, once and for all time that summer, to go to don Celso Villalón's ranch. A goatherd for the summer. And who did I see crossing the street but my uncle-in-law, Juan Briones, on an ice delivery:

"Hullo, boy; dirty laundry?"

Grin. "No sir. I'm off to don Celso's ranch. Could you let Aunt Chedes know of my whereabouts?"

He reached into his pants' watch fob and handed me a dollar bill and a quarter to go with it. "Off to Relámpago, is it?"

"No, not really; to the ranch. Tell her I'm doing all right . . . and how's Vicky? The kids?" '

A shake of the head and a smile. "Up to no good, I imagine."

We shook hands and then he chipped off a piece of ice.

"Here, Jehu."

"You take care, Unc."

He waved and then took on a 100-lb. block and held it as if holding a lunch bag.

A Bit of This, A Pinch of That

Now, since Klail City is like most of the world, fairly con-
servative, one will find that it has kept part of the original city
park and that it has moved the kiosk a bit off center since the
city's incorporation years ago. The park had been there before the Klails came, of course; it'd been laid out by the
original colonials. The land had been set aside as a park under the provision of the *municipio* when the land was in Mexican hands (pre-1845), and then when the Texas and other
Anglos came on down to the Valley in force, they thought it
would be a good idea to leave the park right where it was.
And they did, for a while.

The park, with four wrought-iron gates, (NSEW) lies close
to the railroad depot. The trains run once in a while and when
they do, it's to ship out the agricultural products grown in the
region. The Texas Anglos don't enjoy the park much, and not
at all at night. The Texas Mexicans do, day and night; a
matter of choice and culture.

The park also serves as a regular meeting place for political
speeches, of all things. The politicians take advantage of the
ready-made audience there, and it was there, years ago, and
in another life, that Rafe Buenrostro, Young Murillo, and I
went to see and hear Big Foot Parkinson who was running
again for reelection as sheriff of Belken County.

At the barbershop owned by Chago Solís and Chago Ne-
grete, it was said that Big Foot could barely read, let alone
write his own name; that he was duller than the average
mother-in-law; that the Cookes, the Blanchards, and the
Klails ran him like a setter; that the meat at the political
barbecues was as rotten as they all were; that being dumb
would've helped him were it not for the fact that he was stu-
pid; that he'd turn every which way first chance he got, and
on and on. Like that.

Polín Tapia (poet, painter, and petty politician) also worked as a coyote at the court house, and he'd work and milk whatever victim got in his way. What Young Murillo, many years later, called an Affirmative Action Crook. As time went on (a useful phrase), Polín bought himself a portable Underwood, and he'd use it to write political speeches in Spanish for the Texas Anglo candidates. The Texas Mexicans would listen to any damfool who'd read something off in Spanish and right off they'd claim that Mister So-and-So spoke Spanish, was raised with the mexicanos de Texas, and that he knew the mexicanos, and loved them, understood them, *and* etc.

Big Foot had hired Polín Tapia ad hoc for the primaries; Big Foot usually talked only at barbecues (where people eat, drink and seldom hear or listen) and now with Polín in the van, Big Foot was making his debut at the Klail City Park, *el parque*. (It must be said that Polín helped but did not actually write B.F.'s speeches at this time.) Polín, his words, was an adviser, a counsel. As he told any and everyone at the barbershop: "I reminded him that he was to mention the fact that he was married to a Texana, to a México-Texana."

"Yes, Polín, but at that last barbecue he went balls up, and no one knew what the *hell* he was talking about."

"Did you actually write that talk for him, Polín?"

"No! I'm telling you . . . I acted solely in an advisory capacity." In Spanish: Actué solamente en una capacidad consejal.

"Good for you. But what a client, Polín!"

Polín shrugged.

"But, it's like I always say, Polín, God made everything in eight days, but the Anglos got the patents."

"Bull's eye."

"Let's hear it for ol' Big Foot."

"Oh, but didn't he go and stick his foot in his mouth last Sunday; he, ah . . ."

"And what did the Anglos say when they heard him out there?"

"What they always say: Them *mexicanos* over there . . ."

"No, no; what'd they say about Foot?"

"Oh, that . . . well, what they always say: that Big Foot's dog is smarter than he is . . ."

The talking and the slamming went on for a long time and was stopped only when the Chagos told the hangers-on that they'd be closing the shop early because of the doings at the park: Big Foot was making his first speech there, and they were not about to miss *that*.

"Sure," someone spoke up. "Now that Polín is his main source of advice, why, Big Foot's going to show us a thing or two."

"You're wrong there; Foot's a lost cause, I tell you. I mean, penicillin's a wonder drug and all that, but it can't cure *everything*."

"Okay, boys, gotta batten down the hatches here. Jehu, get the broom, and as soon as you're through, turn off the lights, and don't forget to latch the side door. Just hang the keys on the nail; you know where."

"That's right, Jehu, take care a-that nail; we've got Belken County's only candidate for sheriff in Klail tonight."

"Damn tootin' we do!"

"Hooo, some candidate, eh?"

They finally cut the chatter and I grabbed the push broom; the shop was a two-chair affair, and I began by picking up the Klail City Enterprise News and out of the blue I thought of don Celso Villalón and his goat ranch. The itch to move again. I squeezed the shaving towels, rinsed the shaving mugs, and in came my cousin, Rafe Buenrostro.

"I'm just about through here; what's up?"

"How does a snow-cone sound to you?"

"Sounds good to me . . . hey, there's Young Murillo . . . want me to call him, Rafe?"

But Murillo spotted us at the same time and motioned he'd wait for us there, across the street, and then the three of us made for the park.

"Just saw Maggie Farías, Jehu." Young Murillo; bland.

"She alone?"

"Nah; she's got that little brother-a hers . . ."

"Hnh."

I thought on Maggie a while and then on don Celso again. As I did so, I turned to Rafe:

"I've been thinking of going over to don Celso Villalón's ranch, Rafe. Leave Klail for the rest of the summer; what do you think?"

"You can always stay with us, you know. You're family."

"Yeah . . . I don't know."

"Hey, you two . . . come on, let's go see the crowd. I'm pretty sure I saw Maggie Farías over there."

Rafe. "Maybe Fani's with her." Smile.

The royal palms circling the KC park cast long shadows on the politicians' platform; the six-piece band was on its third number and after that they'd quit to make way for the talk. The neighborhood kids hollered and the families enjoyed the visit and threw an occasional glance at the platform. The wives and mothers kept an eye on their daughters.

After the politicians were introduced to the crowd, but before any speeches, the musicians would come on again and the barbecue would be served. Since the poll taxes were bought and paid for, it was a matter of form. Nothing new, then.

We must have been thirteen or fourteen years old at the time; World War II was on, and we looked at our upcoming Freshman year at Klail High as an armed camp; the school was on the Anglo side of town, and one never knew . . . Times were changing because of the war according to the older people—reassuring themselves, most likely—but if so, why was Big Foot Parkinson the perennial candidate?

The band put away its instruments again and lined up with the barbecue crowd as everyone waited for Big Foot to appear. He spoke last and always when the people were good and fed. An hour later, he drove up, Polín Tapia right behind him, and looked for a place to spit; finding none, Big Foot drew out his handkerchief and pretended to cough. He waved away the microphone someone handed to him and there he stood: beaming and wearing a wide, shit-eating grin all over him.

"Migos meos . . . Mah friends . . . first woman I ever marry was a Meskin girl from Bascom and then she went and died on me . . ."

Applause.

Measuring the crowd, grin in place. ". . . I married again—a second time, see?—and again I married a Meskin girl from Bascom, but she too passed on; died, don't you know."

Applause.

"Well, I married for a third time, a Klail City girl this time, and Meskin a-course . . . and then *she* died."

Here and there voices of dissent would be heard, but barely: "You're feedin' 'em shit, you red-neck!"

"They died on purpose, Asshole!"

"Yeah; it's that breath-a yours!"

Now, the Mexicans who'd been bought and paid for would applaud on cue; some'd even try to shush the hecklers to show that at least *they* were educated; decent folk, see?

But Big Foot grinned all the same; it was in the bag. A general round of applause finished it up and the barbecue and beer were served again. Me, I went to say goodbye to Maggie Farías; she'd stood me up the night before, and dumb as I was, and too given the time and the age, I was hurt and sore. One of those things.

But I decided that night to go out to don Celso Villalón's goat ranch to work the rest of that summer and left early the next morning. I went up to my Uncle Andy's place, said goodbye, and then I crossed the street and walked to the Chagos's barbershop the same morning and packed up.

I did see Rafe Buenrostro at Klail High the following September and the following year, too, when his father was murdered. Rafe's brothers, Israel and Aaron stayed at don Celso's ranch for a while until their uncle, don Julián, returned from Mexico.

Don Julián had crossed the River seeking to avenge his brother's death and did so. I heard him tell about it, but there wasn't any drama to it at all. A straight telling of revenge, and my uncle Julián didn't give, or seem to give, importance to it; just something that needed to be done is how he put it.

As for Big Foot, well, he won his reelection as sheriff for Belken County as usual. No opposition whatsoever, and the people ate more barbecue and drank more beer to celebrate the victory.

Coming Home I

It should come as no surprise that Belken County's largest, best known, and certainly most profitable whorehouse is to be found in Flora. Flora people have convinced themselves that they invented sliced bread; this goes for Texas Mexicans and Texas Anglos alike. For their part, the Flora Mexicans have also come to think of themselves as an integral part of the Flora economic establishment. No such thing, of course; at best, they've stopped resisting, have become acculturated, and, delusion of delusions, have assimilated. All this up to a point, of course, but still, they're an energetic folk and hell to deal and live with.

Flora is also the newest of the Valley towns; sprang up during that war the Anglos had between themselves in the 1860's; truth to tell, though, Texas Mexicans fought on both sides of that one. So, Flora was born yesterday and thus not as old as Relámpago or Jonesville or Klail; Klail City's real name is Llano Grande, the name of the grant. (General Rufus T. Klail came down here, took over the name, and then thought he'd swept away the traditions with the change. And so it goes . . .)

Anyway, the Texas Anglo and Texas Mexican citizenry of Flora are identical in many ways: noisy, trust God and give Him credit on Sundays, and believe in cash on the barrelhead from sunup to sundown. They also believe in other important things: leap years, for one. To their credit, Flora is unlike the other Valley towns in other respects and thus so are the mexicanos who live and die there.

As for whorehouses, this is a lamentably recognized universality, but the Flora-ites claim it as a native invention. Just like that: judgment without explanation. To compensate, perhaps, the town of Flora also boasts of more churches per capita than any other Valley town. See? Admittedly, there is a cure for hiccups (water, air, a good scare); for polio (Drs. Salk and Sabin); but there's nothing you can do about stupidity. Takes more than a pill or a shot for that one. But the Flora-ites don't know this, and if they do, they choose to ignore it. Secure, then, in their ways.

Don Manuel Guzmán, Klail's lone mexicano cop, was rolling himself a flake tobacco cigarette as he sat with some of the *viejitos*—the old men; men his age, then. He'd risen from the sidewalk bench, walked to the curb to stand under the corner lamplight. He spit-sealed his roll, lit it, and looked at his pocket watch: ten after twelve; a warm, foggy, December night, when out of the fog and walking straight at him, there came a woman, gun in hand.

Why, it was Julie, a young black whore from Flora. "Mist Manyul . . . c'n I talk to you?" And then: "Mist Manyul, I done shot Sonny . . . shot 'n killed him, Mist Manyul."

Don Manuel nodded, listened some more, and handed her his cigarette. She stared at it as if she'd never seen one before in her life. Don Manuel opened the front car door, and she slipped in and waited for him as he walked over to see the *viejitos* (Leal, Echevarría, and Genaro Castañeda), those old, well-known friends of the former revolutionary.

"What is it? You leaving now?"

"Got to." Pointing with his chin: "I'll see you here in about an hour or so; and if not here, I'll just drive on to Dirty Luke's."

"What'd she do?"

"She says she shot her husband . . . at María Lara's house . . . in Flora."

"She works there, does she?"

"Aha . . . but she lives here, in Klail. I got them a room at the Flats."

"Hmmm. What happened out in Flora this time?"

"You think the pimp held out on her?"

Don Manuel, slowly. "It's possible; I didn't ask her much, and it's probably best to leave her alone for a while."

"I think you're right there, don Manuel."

Old man Leal: "*I* know who she is. Her man works for Missouri Pacific; a switchman, right? Sonny . . . yeah, he plays semi-pro ball for the Flora White Sox . . . . Yeah."

Echevarría: "Now don't tell me he didn't know about his wife workin' over to Flora?"

Don Manuel: "Oh, he knew all right. They've been married five-six years, I'd say."

Castañeda: "Married." Bland.

Leal: "Do black folks marry? Really?" Curious.

Echevarría: "Yeah, I think they do, once in a while." Not sure.

Castañeda: "Man was probably drinking." Abruptly.

Leal: "Why not?" A hunch of the shoulders.

Echevarría: "Yeah, why not?" Resignation.

Castañeda: "Did, ah, did Sonny pull a knife on her?"

Don Manuel: "Yes; that's what she says."

Leal: "How'd she get over *here* from Flora, anyway?" Admiration.

Don Manuel: "Took a bus, she says."

Echevarría: "A bus? There's a lot-a guts in them ovaries, yes*sir*."

Don Manuel: "I'm taking her to jail; I'll go ahead and drive her on over to Flora tomorrow sometime. She killed her man and they're probably looking for her about now. I think it's best she be alone for a while; cry herself to sleep, think about what she's done; sort things out, you know. But, she needs to be left alone for now; she'll have enough to do tomorrow with that Flora crowd, poor thing . . . Look, I'll see you all here or over to Dirty's."

With this, don Manuel got into his car—his, not the city's which didn't provide him with one, anyway—and then drove

113

Julie Wilson to the Klail City workhouse.

"We goin' to jail, Mist Manyul?"

"Yes."

"I din mean to do it, Mist Manyul. I din mean to kill Son . . . you know that, Mist Manyul? But I kill him . . . . Oh, I shot that man . . . . I say, Son, don't you do it . . . I say, you back off now, you hear? But he din back off none . . . . He din 'n I shot him . . . got him in the chest I did 'n he plop down on the bed there . . . . I kill Son, Mist Manyul, an' you know that no one come to the room when I shot him? . . . Oh, I shot him and killed him, Mist Manyul . . . . He was drunk . . . all out drunk Sonny was and then Ijustupandshothim . . . . You taking me to Flora jail, Mist Manyul?"

"Takin' you to Klail City jail, Julie."

"Oh, thank you, Mist Manyul. I don't want to go to no Flora jail tonight, no I don' . . . . You takin' me there tomorrow? That it, Mist Manyul?"

"Yes . . . tomorrow . . . one of my sons will bring you hot coffee tomorrow morning and then I'll take you to Flora."

"Thank you, Mist Manyul . . . . I won't cry no more . . . I up 'n shot that man and he dead and he deserve it . . . he say he gonna cut me an' I say you back off, Sonny, back off . . . don' come over to here, Sonny, but he did and then I did . . . Mist Manyul, can I go to the bathroom now?"

"There's a bowl in the room."

"Oh, thank you, Mist Manyul."

Don Manuel Guzmán drove out to the corner of Hidalgo Street and since his old friends weren't anywhere to be seen, he did a U-turn in the middle of the deserted main street and headed for Dirty Luke's. Beer time was over and now it was time for the coffee crowd to take over. The *viejitos*'d be there, waiting for him, and then he'd take them home, as always.

Tomorrow, early, *mañana muy de mañana*, after bringing

114

Julie a pot of coffee, he'd drive her to Flora; first though, he'd stop at María Lara's place and get some firsthand news.

He and María Lara had known each other for over forty years, and although there'd been an arrangement between them when both were in their twenties and healthy and vibrant and ready-to-go, their long friendship and a shared place of provenance (the Buenrostro family's Campacuás Ranch) was what kept them in close contact. He thought of the old ranch house and its Texas Ranger-burned-down-to-its-ashes church . . . The ashes were still there, fifty years later. The man shook his head slightly.

But now, headed for Dirty Luke's, he parked any old way and walked into the place; he sat and waited for Rafe Buenrostro to bring him his cup of coffee.

"Boy, turn the volume down; you're going to have the neighbors down on you."

"Yessir."

Coffee over, don Manuel says: "Going back to Hidalgo and First; when y'all get ready to go home, let me know."

The oldsters thank him, as always, and don Manuel leaves the car in front of Dirty's; he's going for a walk, and he'll eventually wind up on Hidalgo Street in Klail City; a town like any other in Belken County in Texas's Lower Rio Grande Valley.

Coming Home II

Easiest thing in the world. Once you've crossed your first river, the rest come easier. Women tell me it's the same thing with husbands: bury the first and so on.

Viola Barragán is one of the chosen; she's crossed rivers, seas, gulfs, oceans, as the saying goes. And, she's buried more than two husbands.

Here we go. Viola Barragán's first husband was the Resident Alien Agustín Peñalosa, a surgeon certified by Mexico City's own Autonomous University, and a northener by birth. A *norteño* from Agualeguas, Nuevo León, he was a resident of Klail City when he died at the hands of an apprentice pharmacist right here in Klail.

It happened that some hysterical biddy (sic Viola) had died while under the care of Dr. Peñalosa, and the husband (widower, really) stated, claimed, and maintained that Dr. P. was to blame; pure and simple, he said; as if things usually turn out p. and s.

Still, the woman *had* died and Dr. Agustín Peñalosa of the Autonomous had been there when Helisa (note the H.) Lara de los Santos joined the other side. (The truth über alles: people who knew her said it was no great loss. A terrible thing to say, but one can always rely on people to say something.)

Now, when Severo de los Santos (the husb.) came calling, the former military surgeon said that the prescription he recommended was the proper one; and he was sniffy about it, too. He then went on to say that the death (which also grieved him, he said) may have been due to something else, and that Señor de los Santos could have his word on *that*.

Señor de los Santos rolled his eyes and was about to rebut when Dr. Peñalosa opened up (figuratively) with some small arms fire. He, sir, was a surgeon, licensed and certified. Furthermore, his professional competence was as unquestioned as was his scientific learning, and thus he *could* and *would* swear that the prescription—*that* prescription—was the proper one. Take that!

The widower mumbled what sounded like sure, sure, but that aside, he then yelled out: But Helisa's as dead as a rotten tooth, and there's no getting her out-a the ground, is there?

Well, things had to come to a head and so Dr. Agustín Peñalosa took Severo de los Santos by the elbow and led him to the pharmacy. The doctor requested an identical prescription, and he wanted it done then and there, in front of the widower and a growing crowd of those not-so-innocent-bystanders who can smell trouble for miles around.

The young apprentice read the prescription, nodded, and began to mix this with that and with that over there, etc. Serious as hell, of course, after all there was an audience and audiences like for the performers to be serious about their business.

Another nod from the apprentice and with a "Here you are, sir," he placed the small bottle in the doctor's hand and then began returning the bigger bottles to their resp. shelves as he worked on other prescriptions.

Dr. Peñalosa held up the vial for de los Santos's view, de los Santos nodded, and the doctor, smiling, gulped it down. There! The former military surgeon shrugged his shoulders, turned toward the door, and then dropped like a stone (broke his glasses and everything) right there on the terrazo floor.

Deader'n goat shit, someone whispered. Man had kicked the bucket and a bystander, and there he was: laid out.

The smile turned into a sneer and his eyes, popped open as they were, began taking a slow, evil look about them. Dead.

"See? What'd I tell you? Well? Just like my Helisa. See?"

The onlookers came in a rush, but not too damn close since Death is contagious, as we say. And then, some public spirit said: "The wife . . . ah . . . widow. Somebody go run and tell her."

Note: No one bothered or blamed the apprentice pharmacist, Orfalindo Buitureyra, son-in-law of Marco Antonio Sendejo, owner and sole prop. of The Future Pharmacy. No need to look for fault, either: the doctor's own mistake, said the witnesses. The result was the same in both cases, and when push does come to shove, one can always settle for a tie.

It turned out that Viola Barragán was out of pocket, so to speak. She was out to Ruffing, visiting her parents: don Telésforo Barragán and his bargain of a wife, doña Felícitas Surís de Barragán, alias Al Capone. Somebody, and it must have been The Voice of Klail City, Gabino Aguilar, drove on out to Ruffing with the news.

The first river Viola Barragán crossed was that old, tired meanderer, the Río Grande. A child in her father's arms she was; Telésforo had said, "The hell with it" during one of the stages of the Mexican Revolution and jumping the Río, family in tow, landed in Klail City where they settled down.

Later on, Viola crossed other rivers, seas, etc. in the company of husband number two:

Karl-Heinz Schuler, an attaché to the German Consulate in Tampico, and who then was appointed first secretary to the Reichminister posted to India.

Brief detour and explanation: Between that shocker at the pharmacy and her marriage to the sainted Karl-Heinz, Viola hooked up (an expression) with don Javier Leguizamón, a more than middle-aged merchant, contrabandista, and Texas Anglo vote getter, buyer, and counter.

All of this is true, of course. The Leguizamón *familia* has a piebald history and as interesting as Hell itself must be, but this is not the time to tell it.

L'affairé Barragán-Leguizamón lasted about a year, give or

take, or, up to the tíme Viola was jettisoned in favor of that green-eyed flash, Gela Maldonado who's stopped a heart or two . . . You must understand that Viola wasn't what we call a mudpie, but she *was* nineteen, and Gela, ah, Gela! she was ten years older, and as fine a piece of nonrustable iron as has ever been made.

As time went on, Viola got to be as firm as Gela, but she had been in need of seasoning and a bit of honing here and there; that was all.

On the economic side, the widowed Viola wasn't the richest woman in Belken County, but she wasn't standing out in the cold on some bread line or other. And, *she* wasn't about to be chased for some eight hours everyday behind some counter or other; no sir. What she did do, was to look around and one day (for no recorded reason) she crossed the Mo-Pac railroad tracks which cleave Klail City in two parts (Anglo Klail from Mexican Klail) and from there, directly to the Belken Bus Line station. She bought herself a round-tripper to Jonesville-on-the-Río. (She had the time and the money but no idea why she had decided to make the trip.) What happened that day is verifiable history: she and the German careerist from Ulm met up on the bus, sat together, talked, boarded off and grabbed another bus back to Klail on the spot.

The Bavarian asked for Viola's hand that very day; the Barragáns stared at that apricot-colored face and nodded their assent, right there and right then. It was all very stiff and formal, and the Barragáns just loved it. Soon after, Karl-Heinz took Viola to Tampico and due to his own talents, Herr Schuler was promoted to first sec. to the Minister, as said.

Talk about happy endings! But, there are those infernal *buts* to deal with. In this case, the *but* was World War II. There's no need to reprise that September 1 all over again, so, en bréve, here's what happened to these two: the Schulers were first interned at an English concentration camp on the outskirts of Calcutta; right after the heat of the season, some bureaucrat decided to transfer three hundred German and Italian consulate and etc. personnel to the homeland of the original concentration camps: South Africa, and there went this Texas Mexican girl up the gangplank on her way to Pretoria.

It must be said that Karl-Heinz was a bulwark. Loyal, faithful, and patiently waiting for the war to come to an end, which it did. He'd been thinking, too. Viola got the news of the Japanese surrender and hung on to her man who remained as calm and placid as a bog. After their release, finally, Herr unt Frau Schuler boated back to the Fatherland.

A longish period of suffering and deprivation followed until the German bureaucracy straightened itself and the occupying forces as well. And, asked Karl-Heinz, what are friends for? The man did have connections, after all, and decided that his future lay with Volkswagen Werke, and that was it. The man was right; and by 1950, he was running the dealership in Pretoria. And, oh, was there money to be made in those days . . . Ho! It rained down on 'em.

And then, with success having moved into the guest bedroom, as it were, Karl-Heinz Schuler died of a massive myocardial infarct. Bad, of course but the family money was untouched by the doctors and hospitals. A blessing from the gloom. And here she was, this Texas Mexican girl, back in Ulm, in a solid brick house and garden living just six blocks from Mannfred Rommel (son and heir of the Feldmarschall) and tending to the elderly Schulers who loved this tall, short-haired, spirited widow who'd married their only son. In their opinion, he'd made a splendid choice for a partner.

Time passed and some years later, the elderly Schulers, in their eighties now, passed on, one right after the other and again Viola took charge: two magnificent coffins, four-dark horses clopping auf dem Friedhof, in this case, the Catholic one in Ulm. And she remained there for another three years until she decided to return home, to Texas, our Texas. But it was a different Viola, close to forty, and monied: she had her husband's insurance, retirement from the Bonn government, the sale of the house, her own solid stock from VW, and money from Wilhelm and Heidi Schuler who left it all to Viola, as they should have. More importantly, Viola also had with her a fine sense and nose for business.

Rich but lonely, so, it was back to Belken County for Viola Barragán. Yes, a different Viola, one who had traveled, and seen, and learned, and profited, too. Aside from that trifling affair with Pius V Reyes at the Holiday Inn, which is another story for another time, Viola married another piece of money: Harmon Gillette. (Rafe Buenrostro and I worked at his print shop during our University summers. Years later, I landed my first solid job at Klail City Savings and Loan upon her recommendation. But that, too, is another story.)

Coming Home III

Damián Lucero (ecce home) makes his living burying the dead and their secret sins.

He has practiced his craft (his own words) in various Valley towns: Relámpago, Flora, Klail City, Ruffing, Edgerton, et alii. This is his third time around for the Texas Mexican cemetery in Bascom. Indeed, counting the Texas Anglo cemetery in Jonesville, Damián Lucero has buried hundreds—thousands—of his fellow Texas Mexicans in Belken County. Sad to say and truth to tell, Lucero has buried friends as well, but he's a pro and carries on like a trouper.

He was born in Relámpago, not too far from the western edge of the el Carmen Ranch; that is, the Buenrostro lands.

"We know that."

Por favor! Lucero, by the way, is his mother's name. The putative . . .

"Putative? Hey!"

. . . the putative father drowned on a lovely autumn dawn as he tried his best to get a tractor, a heavy-duty John Deere, (They're Reliable!) across the Río Grande. One of those fast swirling eddys, sure; that old Río's full of them.

As said, Lucero grew up in Relámpago, and he didn't budge till he was twenty-one years old or so; he got into the shoveling business by luck or chance, one. (It was also the first thing that turned up by way of work.) After the first half-dozen burials, there was nothing to it. A fast learner, then. He bought himself the necessary tools and he also learned to put on a sad, serious face. As for the rest (drive, ambition, muscle, and a will that could bore through limestone), that part is genetic; born with it, see?

"We know what genetic means, Jehu."

And I'll tell you this, too: he's the one who buried Alejandro Leguizamón; that's right. Remember when they buried him; remember where he died? Where he was found? Right on Sacred Heart Church property? Well, there he was, and he had one of those heavy tire irons for a hat. Damn thing went right through his skull, bone and everything. Well, old Alejandro, he was taken to the Texas Anglo mortuary home in Klail, but he was buried in the Mexican cemetery in Klail; the new one. Alejandro never knew this, did he? A closed affair it was 'cause, try as they might, no mortician alive could remove that God-given sneer a-his. Man was born that way, like he was always smelling bad air.

"You mean *farts*, don't you?"

I mean *bad air* and we'll let it go at that. Anyways, that was some funeral, wasn't it? I mean, thousands of people showed up for that one and *everybody* brought flowers. Seemed like an insult, all those flowers, and probably meant that way, too . . . . At any rate, Alejandro Leguizamón left a lot of friends and enemies in Belken County; a lot of both.

Lucero says that over to Jonesville, at the Texas Anglo cemetery, they paid him by the week not by the customer. Regular, then; not much more than anywhere else, you understand, but it was by *check*. Yeah. A check has more *vista*, huh?, more importance than real money, sometimes, yeah . . . . Now, as far as Jonesville is concerned again, Lucero says that one grave digging and funeral stands out; tops. Turned out to be that Chief-a-Police's woman; no, not his wife, you understand. *La Colorada*, the redhead. She was a big old thing. Blew into Jonesville from somewhere Up North; Houston, maybe . . . Blew in and baited, hooked, and landed old Popeye Dieckemann faster 'n you can say Hernán Cortez—provided you *can* say Hernán Cortez.

Big funeral . . . she's the one who crashed into one of those girders at the International Bridge, on the American side; man, she burst like a pink grapefruit. Oooh!

Lucero says that Texas Anglo cemeteries are *escuetos*—bereft of adornment.

"Bereft? Say . . ."

Ok, ok, ok. Anyway, few flowers at those cemeteries; no crosses to speak of, and they go ahead and manicure—look here, that's what Lucero says—they go ahead and manicure the lawns; yeah. And how do they know who's buried where? Well, for that there's a little marker flush with the ground: name, date of birth, year of death, and—once in a while—a Beloved Son or a Beloved Father, but that's about it. Bereft.

Well, one time, out to Edgerton I think it was, a man came up to him saying he had a special request: he had a lodge brother Woodman of the World to bury, but he wanted him standing up.

"And you'd like him straight up, that it?"

"On his two feet, yessir."

"And you want the hole to be a round one . . . like for a barbecue, right?"

"Aha! Only deeper, of course."

"Rounder . . . and deeper. Okay. And your lodge brother? Was he a tall one?"

"Well, no, not too much . . . kind-a short like."

"Short. Like me?"

"Well, no again; not that short. Somewhere between you and me, let's say."

"Aha . . . Well, where is he now?"

"We put him over to the Vega Brothers."

"And he's all fixed up 'n everything; ready to go? I mean, he's been *prepped*, has he?"

"Oh, yeah, I think so . . . . And, ah, this is okay with you, right? I mean . . . it's no inconvenience, the burying straight up?"

"No sir; not at all. I'll do the digging, and . . . excuse me, is there going to be a lot of people here?"

"No; it's a kind of closed funeral, if you know what I mean; me, my two brothers, a cousin or two, some close friends, a few lodgemen . . . Small. Why do you ask?"

"It's the ah . . . the originality of it, see? I mean, some people are just naturally curious, ye-know."

"I wouldn't worry about it. Think you can have the hole ready by this afternoon . . . six o'clock?"

"On the dot. Was, ah, your lodge brother, was he the chunky type?"

"No. Regular, if anything."

"Regular. Thank you, I'll have the cross, and . . ."

"No. No cross. Nothing of the sort . . . we're planning to bring him something ourselves, later on."

"O—kay . . . how's about an arrow, like a marker?"

"Yeah; that'll do it."

Well, that dead party looking out to the world was a man named Fidencio Anciso, and it was his idea to be buried that way . . .

"Aw, go on, Jehu . . .I find that one kind-a thick to swallow without any water to go with it."

It's the truth, though. I tell you who else he buried: Pius V. Reyes.

"Yeah! He's the one they found in the Holiday Inn . . . isn't that right?"

"Oh, yeah . . . I remember now. Old Sure-shot."

"Sure-shot? Why?"

" 'Cause he was a stud, that's why . . . see a woman, make a beeline, and there he went. Never missed."

"He must've missed now and then; he and his wife never had any kids."

"And what's that got to do with anything? That was their affair. He made out like a banker, really."

"You wouldn't know it to look at him."

"I'll say."

"Well, *I* find it hard to believe. You, Jehu?"

Pius V was buried over to Bascom . . . the Mexican Protestant Cemetery. Presbyterians, they were.

"Jehu's right. It rained that day, too."

"I remember . . . and a norther blew in."

"They related, Jehu?"

Who?

"Why, Pius V and the gravedigger?"

No; not as far as I know. Why?

"And who was it they buried standing up, Jehu?"

A man named Anciso . . . Fidencio Anciso from Carrizal Ranch.

"And why standing up? Of all things . . ."

"In Belken? Anything is possible in Belken. Shoot."

Well, he may have been from Flora for all I know.

"Now you're talking; talk about crazies . . ."

"Speaking of the devil . . ."

"What? Where?"

Like Leal says, speaking of the devil: there's Lucero himself.

(Sure enough, the gravedigger is walking up Klail Avenue; a slow walk, measured kind-a, a bit stiff, turns his head, spots the group, moves his head in greeting, and now crosses the street to say hello.)

"Afternoon, Jehu."

Afternoon.

"How's it going?"

"What's up?"

"Working hard?"

"Oh, so, so. ¿Qué pasa aquí?"

"Just talking."

"Yeah? What about?"

"Oh, this and that . . . Jehu here told us about a guy you buried standing up one time."

"Well, I sure did . . . one-a the Ancisos. Yeah."

"That's what Jehu said. But why standing up?"

"Well, that's what Anciso himself wanted . . ."

"*Some* people . . ."

"But, ah, how did you all place the floral arrangements without a cross to hang 'em on? I mean, those rounded ones with the ribbons and all."

"There were a few a-those, all right, but we sort of stacked them up, one-a top-a the other . . . . It looked kind-a strange to me . . . . I'll tell you this, I was afraid people'd start making all kinds of requests after that one, but it didn't turn out that way a-tall. People are more traditional than you think. Up to now, he's the only one. A-course, I did charge 'em more."

"Oh?"

"Well, the digging took a bit of doing, see?"

"And the covering?"

"Naw, that wasn't too bad; just took some extra tamping down for that. Tell you this too, though, some of the people there heard the slumping and bumping. Right, Jehu?"

Laugh.

"What does he mean, Jehu?"

He's right. We had to go from North to South, right? Straight up. You know, on end? Well, it turned out that the Vega brothers didn't strap him down, so when the coffin was placed up, old Fidencio Anciso slumped. Coffin was made of wood, so we heard him.

"Is that *true*?"

"Like Jehu just said . . . anyway, we just lowered him into that hole, and we commenced to cover him up right smart. Jehu here was an acolyte, and they *all* heard the body shift, see? Nobody laughed, although they sure were looking at each other. Good thing nobody laughed; laughing would-a ruined it. Well, sir, covering him was easier, like I said . . . oh, a bit of rounding off, but pretty level, considering."

This Anciso was called Bald-pate; Bald-knob. Knobby . . . something like that. Wore a wig, see?

Lucero: "Yes, he did. A hair piece. A toupee."

"And you-all buried him, hair piece and all?"

"Yep; it was stuck there."

"*Some* people!"

"Yeah. Hair piece and all. A bit of a problem,though. The damn thing kept slipping off, the Vegas said, but they fixed that, all right: took a itty-bitty tack and a peen hammer, and plinkstayed on, after that."

"Jay-sys! Why'n't ye-use a paste or something?"

"All there was; you got to make do sometimes . . . improvise."

Other deaths and burials, and the people were the same: friends, relations, neighbors. As for Lucero, he says one orifice is the same as any other: the one which gives life or the one which cuts it off.

Lucero doesn't stop to ponder metaphysical questions, if the one just posed is metaphysical; it could be existential for all Sartre and I know. The point is that Lucero doesn't look into the how or the why of it all; he has his eyes on the whom and the where. Less problems that way, he says.

Damián Lucero, like the rest of us, seldom thinks about his own burial. It could be, it just *could* be, that he too would like to be buried standing up. Why not?

Coming Home IV

Today, a nice, hot, cloudless summer day and no different from any other for this time of year in Belken County, the Klail City mexicano neighborhood came to pay its last respects (a manner of speaking) to don Epigmenio Salazar; Father Efraín led the procession on its walk to the mexicano cemetery in Bascom.

Epigmenio, in life, had been a loyal consort (acc. to his lights), a stalwart paterfamilias (to Yolanda, m. to Arturo Leyva, a bookkeeper), and a straight, upright *hombre de bien*. This, according to that bookkeeping son-in-law of his, would be an entry on the Asset side of the ledger; the barbers, however, when it came to the upright, straight, etc., part, said that this too was a manner of speaking since the man's king-sized hernia forbade erectness. The hernia was a lifesaver: Don Epigmenio stopped working for a living on the day following his marriage to doña Candelaria Murguía de Salazar aka La Turca.

Epi was a bit of a shit (my cousin Jehu, here) who smooched drinks and cigarettes; he also stretched the truth here and there.

On balance, then, this falls on he left side, the Debit side of the ledger.

Years ago, in the important field of Geopolitik, he sided with the Axis Powers; a great admirer of the Herrenvolk, esp. in '40–42 when the Allies were getting shut out; he put his money where his mouth was, though, so to speak. His faith in the B.R.T. Axis was such that when the time came for his grandchild's baptism, Epigmenio was in a quandary. What to do? What to name the child? Kesselring? Rommel?

Don Efraín, the priest, brought him up short:

"What? Those heretics?"

"Strategists, don Efraín; not heretics."

"Stay out of this, Epigmenio. Well, Arturo? Yolanda?"

Epigmenio, again, and for a last try: "How about Adolf?"

"Like the Führer?"

"Yes, exactly."

"Dear God! Come on, you two, what name have you come up with?"

"Arturo Junior, like his Dad."

"That's better; Epigmenio, you hush."

And Epigmenio hushed, but not forever: instead, he got even. From that day on he called his grandson Rommel, flat out. The kid, no dummy, answered to Rommel as he grew up.

"Rommel, here's a dime; go get me a copy of *La Prensa*, and get yourself an ice cream cone or something."

"Rommel, my boy, have you heard the one about the deaf priest and the parrot?"

"Rommel, you keep that up, and there'll be no movies for a week."

Arturo Jr. sized up the character he had for a grandfather, but, in the end, they wound up close friends. Another fact: his friends at school also called him Rommel later on. The truth is that he didn't look like the Feldmarschall at all; the truth also is that his friends had no idea who Rommel was, if indeed, he had been somebody.

There was no beating don Epigmenio at being the first with the news. It was he, and no one else, who solved the riddle as to the sudden disappearance of the girl clerk at the pharmacy, a mystery which had baffled and preoccupied some of the soundest minds in Klail City. She had left on the bus and on her own, too. Pure and simp.

Oh, the cook at the Phoenix Cafe had tried a bit o' this and a bit o' honey, but she wasn't having any. Marriage or nothing, she'd said, and then she'd bought that Greyhound ticket for Chicago. Of all places. (The Klail Citians had said otherwise: pregnant, for sure; not a virgin, so *who* wants her? No, she's frigid, that's what's the matter. Etc.)

All wrong, of course; she had gone to Chicago. Had a sister who got her a job, and that was it.

Epigmenio said he'd been the first to remove whatever stain had fallen on her. Some kind souls reminded him that he'd placed the stain there in the first place.

Oh, that?

"Well, upon gathering all the facts and data (he said) I did what any general would do: I reviewed the situation, covered my flanks, and increased my patrols; that's all."

Clear-eyed and clear-speaking neighbors is something we have in Klail City and some were forward enough to say that Epigmenio sucked wind up his ass. Plain-speaking neighbors are liable to speak that way, by the way.

The four stalwart Garrido brothers were charged with lowering Epigmenio and his casket, and the brothers did it as they've done it for so many times: with an air of studied indifference, as it were.

Doña Candelaria Murguía de Salazar stopped them at the midway point: "Hold on to the ropes, boys." She gathered two scoops of the freshly turned loam: "Epigmenio, you drone, it's a beautiful day, cloudless, hot, and not a hope of rain. It's June, Epi, and now your friends and I are here to see you off; what more could you possibly hope for?"

Doña Candelaria turned to the oldest of the Garridos.

"Cayetano, I'll start him on his way," and she let the hot dirt slide from her hands. "You be damned sure he's covered well, you hear? Adiós, Epigmenio."

But it was all show. Inside, in that flinty heart of hers, the widow Candelaria missed her husband. My Drone, and no one else's, she'd say.

Coming Home V

Don Orfalindo Buitureyra

is a quadrilateral lump of Valley loam and shit. Buitureyra is also a pharmacist, thanks to some pretty lax laws in the Lone Star State; there are other weaknesses in Orfalindo Buitureyra's arsenal: he's a sentimentalist and so much so that he goes on three-four day drunks (we call 'em *parrandas serias*), and then, later on, he wonders where those King Kong-sized hangovers come from; as said, forgetful, as most sentimentalists.

Anyway, the man will break out two or three times a year and here's the pattern: he'll drink alone for a while, and then he'll drink with some friends, and *then* comes the dancing (a solo effort) and then la piéce de résistance: He sings.

"I like to," he says. To tell the truth, he's so-so in that department.

On the other hand, there's no oratory, no public crying, declamations, patriotic speeches, etc. "That's for queers; get me?"

Sure, sure, don Orfalindo; no need to come to blows over a little thing like that, is there?

"Good! Just so's we understand each other. Know what I mean? Now, where was I?"

Singing.

"Right! Almost forgot . . ."

And he does. Actually, what he does is to sing along with the Wurlitzer. The following is tacit: if an Andalusian *paso doble* breaks out, the floor belongs to don Orfalindo. The reader probably thinks people stop and stare; the reader is *wrong*. And no, it isn't that the drinkers are bored stiffer than the Pope; not at all. It's more like this: live and let live. Man wants to dance? Let him. Man wants to dance alone? Who's he bothering? Right!

To put it as plainly as possible: People simply leave him alone.

"They'd better; what if he poisons them, right?"

Jesus! I'd forgotten about that . . .

"Tscha! I'm just talking."

Don Orfalindo Buitureyra, it so happens, is a cuckold. A *cabrón*, a capricorn, antlered. You with me? This makes him the lump he is. And, he's a nice old guy, too. None of this is incompatible, and why should it be? A bit of a fool, like all of us, then, *but* he *is* a cuckold; in his case, a cuckold Made in Texas by Texas Mexicans.

"And the kids?"

"Oh, they're his, all right."

"Damn right they are: they got his nose, all-a them."

"And that lantern jaw, too; even that girl a-his has it."

"Hmmm; but he's a *cabrón*, and that stain won't go away."

"We—ell now, that's something that don't rub off with gasoline. Goes deeper than that, you see."

This is all talk. Don Orfalindo is, *a la italiana*, *cornutto*, but not *contento*. If anything, he's resigned to it. A bit of Islamic resignation that.

"Look, his kids like him and love 'im. Isn't that enough?"

"Yeah, what the hell. Tell me this: just how long is that wife a-his gonna remain good looking? There's no guarantee of longevity, you know."

"Well, nothing lasts one hundred years, not even a man's faith, let alone his wife. Truth to tell, though, he'll wear those horns to his grave."

"How long she been running around now? Five? Six years? Give her two, three more; tops."

"Well, Echevarría you ought to go into counseling and fortune-telling, ha!"

"Tscha! A matter of time, is all. Look at him: dancing that *Silverio Pérez* paso doble . . . Who's he bothering?"

"Well now, if it comes to bothering, you're right: he's not bothering anybody, but look out in the sidewalk there: there's some youngster watching him."

"So? Those aren't his kids; his are all grown up."

A newcomer said that; and he really doesn't belong in that table with the *viejitos*: "Out with it, then . . . who's his wife fooling around with?"

This is a breach; the inquisitor should know better.

The Wurlitzer blinked once or twice and then some *norteño* music came on: don Orfalindo went to the bar.

Not a peep at the table. Don Orfalindo's at the bar and orders another Miller Hi-Life. The men at the table look away, and the inquisitor excuses himself; to the john, he says.

Don Orfalindo takes a swig from the Miller's and then, without fail, he caps the bottle with his thumb. Conserves the carbonation, he says.

The *viejitos* at the table wave; he waves back. They're all friends; good men, really. The man who went to the john is still out there. It's hoped he doesn't ask many more questions. What would be the use?

First of all, being a cuckold isn't a profession; it's hard, cruel, but then it can happen to anybody: Napoleon, the President of the United States, one's best friend. No telling. There's don Orfalindo, for ex. Except for the oldsters at the table, few know and less remember *the reason* for don O.'s binges. As my neighbor says: "Who cares?"

"Don Manuel Guzmán ought to be dropping in pretty soon."

"Right as rain. Rafe! Rafe, boy, better heat up that coffee;

don Manuel ought to be coming in any minute now."

"Yessir."

Don O. pulls away from the bar; on his way to the john. But here comes the Grand Inquisitor; they almost run into each other.

At the table, Esteban Echevarría, Luis Leal, don Matías Uribe, and Dirty Luke, the owner of the place, throw a glance at the pair. The four men, the *viejitos*, shake their heads; the inquisitor shouldn't even be at this table, he's forty years old and out place with these men. He invited himself, then. Worse, it's don Manuel's chair.

Enter don Manuel. "Son, cut the volume you're going to get the neighbors down on you."

Don Orfalindo is back at the bar, bottle in hand, thumb in cap. He spots don Manuel at the table.

"Begging your pardon, don Manuel, but I've been drinking."

"You want me to take you home, don Orfalindo?"

"Well, no; ah . . . not this minute. I just started this morning."

"Well, you take care now."

"Yessir; I'm going back to the bar now."

There'll be no dancing by don Orfalindo as long as don Manuel is in there. (A note of respect acc. to don O.) For his part, don Manuel sips at his coffee and, as he finishes, says to the others: "My car's out front; let me know when you're ready to go." He rises and walks out the front door.

The inquisitor is back, too, but the chair is no longer there.

As don Manuel walks out, don Orfalindo hits the floor: *Besos Brujos* (letra de R. Schiammarella; con música de Alfredo Malerba). Libertad or Amanda sings out: "Déjame, no quiero que me beses . . ."

Un tango, tangazo! Eyes closed, don Orfalindo Buitureyra glides away. Years, miles, and more years: it's that woman again: young, hardbodied, once married to a former military surgeon from Agualeguas, Nuevo León; the surgeon died as a result of a prescription handed him by the apprentice pharmacist Orfalindo Buitureyra years and years ago . . .

Besos Brujos; bewitched kisses, in English, doesn't cut it. Another long glide by the man and *then* a sudden severe cut to the right! *Bailando con corte*! Eyes closed, harder now. A smile? Is it? Yes!

The eyes remain closed. Yes; he smiles again, and one could almost say, almost say, that don Orfalindo Buitureyra is contented enough to be happy. And alive, and older, too.

But above all, happy; *y eso es lo que cuenta*. And that's what counts.

A Classy Reunion

The Homecoming

"Apple core!"
"Baltimore!"
"Who's your friend?"
"Elsinore!"

There she is, Elsinore Chapman, holding a glass of New
York Taylor; but that's not the Elsinore I see at the moment.
No. I'm looking at the fifteen-year-old Elsinore Chapman
who's guarding, blocking, my way to the Klail City High
School Library. She's been given strictest orders: a six-week
banishment for me. Loud talk in Spanish—or so says Miss
Mary Jane McClarity. Poor things.

"How's the champagne, Jehu?"

The fifteen-year-old Elsinore hasn't the vaguest that
twenty-three years later she'll have married, divorced, and
that she and I will have been colleagues for a while at Klail
High. And, she'll have a daughter, too; a kid named Birdie
(named for some maternal grandmother named Birdwell), and
both Elsinore and her dau. will trace and follow similar foot-
steps as Elsinore's parents: living in a nice, cool, quiet household where courtesy takes precedence over warmth. It
happens.
At Klail High, the teen-age Elsinore is big buddies (her
words) with Molly Loudermilk (who'll marry as well and
have two-three kids) and with Liz Ann Moore who'll marry
once, twice, and then marry for keeps to someone who
1. puts up with her; 2. understands her; 3. loves her; and
4. who'll know that the one she *really* loved was someone

else, a classmate erased in a bloody car wreck about the time Liz was on husband No. 1. Both Molly and Liz Ann live in Houston now, and they'll run across each other once in a while. But only just.

We're all here at the Twenty-Second Class Reunion; a Klail High homecoming . . .

Two other close friends of Elsinore, Belinda Braun and Lulu Gottlieb, will disappear into America's Melting Pot. Belinda will wind up teaching math at Klail High and will marry a milkman, Ned Parks. A brother of the milkman (a Phillips 66 lessee) will marry Lulu Gottlieb; a friendly, smiling type, Lulu. (In high school she always had a smile on and so we voted for her in the high school elections.)

Explanation: Rafe Buenrostro thought it a good idea to write about our graduating class. He never got around to it, and so, I'm filling the void; as it were. Not completely, of course, since the Belken County Chronicles leave much to be filled and desired.

"Canapés? More champagne, you-all?" I turn. Molly Loudermilk. Molly Loudermilk Hall; I stand corrected.

But I'm back at the study hall with Elsinore . . . An exile from the library, from the books, for six weeks. A term. Three seats up and to the right: Domingo and Fabián Peralta, twins of the Belken County Court House coyote, Adrián Peralta. The twins speak English all the time, but I've yet to catch either one of them reading a book. The wily coyote has taught the cubs to smile and to put on a good face.

When Korea came calling, these two were out; missed a big part of their education, then. But they've learned to be sociable and to make small talk. A change, if not an improvement.

The twins didn't go out for athletics either nor would they sit with us on the gym steps. Equity above all else: they didn't sit with our Fellow Texans either. A lone and solitary animal, the coyote . . . But they did have friends: those two standing by the bar. Friends who started school with the coyotes at St. Anne's Parish school. The yessir-yesm'am's and no sir-noma'am's, as Rafe called them.

And there's Rafe listening to Liz Ann Moore; she puts her hand on his shoulder.

Back to the coyotes; their friends are Noé Olmedo and Horacio Navarro. Noé's a pain, but he does have a sister, Fani, who broke my heart in high school: she became a Carmelite. Horacio Navarro (as we say) "counts as much as a nought to the left." These four, the coyote kids and their friends, are ageless; oh, a pound here and there, a sag, a lessening of hair; but that's a physical beating of time.

They wave as I cross the room for a warm hand-holding from an old friend, a new friend, a present friend: Sammie Jo Perkins.

Well, look over there; all smiles. J.D. Longley; oh, yes. Lives in El Campo; Wharton. One of the two. J.D. is the Colonel's son. Old Colonel Longley and his lady got themselves a divorce after all these years. Messy, too. Colonel Longley, don't you see, ran off with their Mexican maid. It happens.

Elsinore waves at me. Motions that we'll be eating in a few minutes.

There's Edwin Dickman talking to J.D. Ed's an orphan; raised by his grandparents; folks died in a . . . I forget. This is their house; about as big as the Bank. And there's Roger Bowman; Ed lives in Bascom, now, and Roger in Edgerton.

First time I met Roger he was riding a Schwinn. Almost ran me over, too. Nothing personal, though: we were both watching the cheerleaders. And there's the clean up hitter in this line up: Robert Stephenson Penwick. Most Handsome, Most Likely to Succeed. *Robin* to those who knew him well. The spreading of smiles all around also got him Best All Around. All this turned out be a future help; he's just finished his term as State President of the Kiwanians, and he's on his third term on the school board. He heads the Klail City Independent Underwriters; a front for the Bank.

"Jehu. Refill?"

Smile. "Thanks, Elsinore."

She smiles. "What-cha thinking about?"

"About the last twenty years . . ."

"Well, be nice now." And off she goes.

And here's Royce Westlake and Harv Moody; cousins. Their fathers married the Ridler sisters, Valerie and Sybil. Methodists, I think. We almost turned Royce down at the Bank this week, but Harv came through with the collateral. Nothing personal.

And, speaking of money, there's Elsinore leading us all to the sit-down dinner with a practiced wave of the hand; that's the same hand that kept me away from the library; oh, well.

There's Molly, waving at Liz Ann Moore and pointing to the door.

And look at *that*! Babs Hadley; late as usual. Had her own car then, too. Used to pick up Charlie Villalón at his dad's goat ranch. Babs is walking this way. A kiss, not a peck.

"You haven't changed, Jehu."

"I've tried, I've tried." Sits next to me, on my right. We go a long way, she and I.

Elsinore. "More champagne? And do try the mushrooms, everyone."

Name tags along the table: Watfell, Posey, Keener, Bewley. What's in a name? Ah, the Hindenburg Line: Muller, Bleibst, Gottschalk, Voigt . . . The poor whites: Watkins, Snow, Allen . . .

And there's Rafe, looking at me again. He motions. Ten minutes. I nod. In ten minutes, somebody, Liz Ann Moore probably, will read the twenty-two-year-old class will.

Graduation night. School board president; a man born to the job. Talks about shoulder to the wheel, nose to the grindstone, ear to the ground.

Hand in your pocket?

The-poor put upon Superintendent passes out the diplomas; a whiff of liquor of some sort. Diplomas in hand, and it'll be the Army for many of us. The Super's son had flat feet, but not so flat that he couldn't play ball up in Boulder, some place. Bobby Thurlow. Talk has been that he's gay; prob. not true and prob. not important either.

Forty-six in our graduating class, and forty remain twenty-two years later. Elsinore sits to my left, next to me; makes it a point. The Peralta twins are at each end of the table. Young Murillo is next to one of them and so is Alfonso V squez. Good for him. Did a little time in Huntsville and now works at a tire store. Young Murillo made himself into an electrician; a contractor, now. Winks.

The Green Gauntlet is the caterer and Roger Bowman is the official master of ceremonies. Out back, everything is lit up and bright as day for us; skeet shooting at night after dinner and drinks.

But who is this across the way? Ah. Ed Dickman's wife. A Valley girl, but no Klail Citian . . . Oh, yes; she's known me (about me) for years. From Ed here, she says. Sure.

Saw Ed a month ago at the Bank; we financed his fifth camera shop in the Valley.

And there's a cousin of mine, Rafael Prado. Stayed in after Korea and traveled all over. Mustanged it to Lt. Col., and brought back a German wife: Hannelore, and now they've got four German-Mexican kinder. He's now a Lt. Col. (Ret.) and a game warden in Flads; County seat of Dellis. Happy, the six of them, and why shouldn't they be?

"Did you hear that Jehu gave up teaching English at Klail High? Yes, he did; he's at the Bank now. Aren't you, Jehu?

You traitor, leaving Klail High for the Bank . . ."

It's Sofía Vergara. And she's with Emma Castro. Who else? Ah, yes. First with Sofía and then with Emma, and then, one day of a Spring month, the three of us skipped school all day long at Emma's house.

Sofía's married to Julio Zavala of Zavala's Television, and Emma married Nestor Reyes . . . nephew to the late Pius V. Reyes who died while resting atop Viola Barragán at the Holiday Inn.

Babs Hadley nudges me a bit. The caterer waits, bottle in hand. Yes, thank you; and he pours.

"Wherever you were just now, Jehu, I wish I'd been there."

Babs. Smiling.

The farm girls are here too: Blanca Aguinaga heads the list. And Conce Guerrero would have been here with Rafe; but she died. Drowned on an Easter Sunday picnic; years ago. And look who came down from Michigan City, Indiana: Dorothea Cavazos; now *she* was a good one. And here's another farm girl: Elodia Cavazos. These two are first cousins; Elodia now lives in Dellis County; a nurse.

There's Julian and Timoteo Vilches. Cousins of Rafe's and mine. Law partners. Julian once held off the white trash long enough for me to come over and help. No big deal. Some of them are at this table; we all laugh about it now. And we should. And we do. Timo points to me and then to Elsinore.

He remembers.

"Can I get you a couple of books, Cousin?" And Timo then brought them out to me that afternoon twenty-odd years ago.

Poor Miss Mary Jane McClarity; using Elsinore as a cop. You're twenty years older, Miss McClarity, wherever you are. I am too, of course, but look at it this way: You're twenty years older than *I* am . . .

And no, it wasn't I who yelled in study hall. Not that time.

"Here, Jehu; this fresh glass is for you. Special."
"Thank you, Elsie."
No pain, no debt, nothing lasts a hundred years.

Apple core!
Baltimore!
Who's your friend?